02

15

HEART ON FIRE

HEART ON FIRE

Iris Gower

This title first published in Great Britain 2000 by
SEVERN HOUSE PUBLISHERS LTD of
9–15 High Street, Sutton, Surrey SM1 1DF.
Originally published 1981 in paperback only under the title
Beloved Traitor and pseudonym of *Iris Davies*.
This title first published in the U.S.A. 2000 by
SEVERN HOUSE PUBLISHERS INC of
595 Madison Avenue, New York, N.Y. 10022.

British Library Cataloguing in Publication Data

Gower, Iris
    Heart on fire
    1. Slaves - Morocco - Fiction
    2. Love stories
    I. Title
    823.9'14 [F]

    ISBN 0-7278-5480-1

Printed and bound in Great Britain by
MPG Books Ltd, Bodmin, Cornwall.

Author's Note

When I first began to write for publication, I was unsure
which direction I wished to pursue. So the reader of this
reprinted novel will find it differs greatly from my currently
published historical books.

In the past I wrote historical romps and Victorian thrillers
and tried my hand at modern romance. These are the books
you will have taken from the shelves if you are reading this
author's note. In spite of the differences from my later
novels, I do hope my readers will find these stories a good
read and a glimpse into the past efforts of the author.

Best wishes to all my readers, old and new.

Iris Gower

CHAPTER ONE

Garnet Kingdom had never been in love. She was past sixteen years of age and should have been betrothed long since but her father was over-fussy, ambitious to make a match worthy of the only child of such a prominent family.

Lord Grosvenor Kingdom, a minister in the new régime of King George the fourth, had latterly been the subject of an assassination attempt. For this reason alone, he had brought himself to part with his daughter and send her on a visit to her Aunt Letticia in Spain.

It had been a joy to Garnet that her trip aboard the *Lady Elizabeth* had coincided with her childhood friend's journey to join her fiancé's regiment, yet as the cool of the English shores faded into the distance, her pleasure had been marred by envy for Caroline Grey's obvious love for her soldier sweetheart. It had served to highlight the lack in her own life.

Garnet turned over restlessly in her bunk, listening to the wind cracking in the sails. Yesterday the ship had docked at Brest to take on fresh supplies and

Captain Treherne had told her that soon they would be sailing past the coast of Portugal.

She sighed, rising to her knees, pressing her face against the window, staring out at the moon-silvered seas. Once the *Lady Elizabeth* reached the straits of Gibraltar, the journey would be almost over. She might catch a glimpse of Caroline's young officer before being whisked away to her aunt's house, see the man who inspired such love.

In a way it would be sad to leave the ship; she had enjoyed the company of Mrs. Treherne and the other English ladies on board who had fussed over and petted her as though she were still a child. Garnet was well aware that her father had given the captain and his wife minute instructions on the care of his daughter as well as a handsome purse, but for all that, the concern shown for her welfare was kindly and, she felt, genuine.

It was becoming increasingly hot in the small cabin. Garnet pushed back the covers and lifted the heavy cloth of her nightgown above her knees. In her hasty packing, no provision had been made for the change in climate. Her garments were all of good quality but thick and unsuitable for such heat.

Caroline, no doubt warned by her young soldier, had been better prepared. She wore the finest of linens and gossamer silk gowns that whispered round her feet as she walked the decks. She had offered to lend Garnet some of her clothes, a most generous gesture but one impossible to accept because of the difference in the stature of the two girls. Caroline was tall, slen-

der as a reed, while Garnet was tiny, though her
breasts and hips were well rounded.

A sudden, unfamiliar sound made Garnet lift her
head and listen intently. A blaze of lights through the
porthole caught her eye and, leaning forward, she saw
another ship approaching swiftly through the darkness of the sea.

There was a sense of eeriness about the vessel
ploughing through the water towards the *Lady
Elizabeth*. Garnet's heart began to beat swiftly in apprehension and, even as she watched, a tongue of
flame shot across the void between the ships.

At once, there seemed to be great confusion on
board. Garnet heard a hoarse voice shouting commands and there was the sound of a shot being fired.
The *Lady Elizabeth* shuddered from stem to stern as the
hostile ship loomed up like a monster, ramming her
mercilessly.

Garnet clung to the bunk in an effort to steady
herself. She was panic-stricken, not knowing if she
should run up on deck or remain in her cabin. The
decision was taken out of her hands as her door was
flung open and she saw the lick and crackle of flames
as the mast began to burn.

Silhouetted against the blaze was a gigantic figure,
a scarlet kerchief tied around grizzled hair. A great
arm reached towards her and her wrist was caught in a
cruel grip. She screamed as she was dragged up on
deck.

The other women passengers were already standing
in a line, faces shocked and white under the fierce glare

of the fire. Mrs. Treherne, her hair hanging in untidy whisps on her shoulders, watched her possessions being tipped out onto the deck before her.

Caroline stood beside her in silent dignity and, as Garnet was thrust forward, she encircled her with her arms as though Garnet were a child who needed protection.

The women were herded towards the edge of the deck and Garnet thought for a moment that the intention was to push them into the blackness of the sea. But strong arms reached out, lifting them, one by one onto the enemy vessel.

'Below!' The great man who had taken Garnet from her cabin gave her a jab with a cutlass and she stumbled as she descended the steps, following the other women into the hold. The hatch was closed above them with a harsh grating sound and Garnet found herself in a deep, smothering darkness. She felt breathless with panic and someone beside her began to sob.

Garnet reached out and her hands encountered the roughness of the timbers. She felt her way along the side of the ship until she came to a cask where she sat, trying to calm herself and accustom her eyes to the gloom.

'Garnet, is that you?' Caroline Grey caught her hands, drawing her close, and they clung together.

'What do you think they mean to do with us?' Garnet asked in a small voice and Caroline took a deep breath.

'I'm not sure, but I hope their captain is more of a

gentleman than are his crew.' Both knew it was un-
likely that the man who had attacked the *Lady
Elizabeth* was anything but a scoundrel. They fell silent
and Garnet knew that her friend must be wondering if
she would ever again see her young officer.

As the time dragged slowly by, the air in the hold
became fetid and Garnet was finding it difficult to
breathe. She leaned against the timbers, smelling the
pitch and the salt of the sea in the rough wood, her eyes
closed, trying not to think too far ahead.

The hatch was dragged open and sunlight splashed
into the hold. Garnet blinked rapidly, straining to see
through the glare. Footsteps pounded heavily down
the stairs and the sailor with the grizzled hair caught
her roughly by the arm.

'Wait!' Mrs. Treherne stepped forward. 'Where are
you taking the girl?' She did not wait for a reply. 'One
of us older ladies should be allowed to speak with your
captain. We have a right to know what he intends
doing with us.'

The man pushed her aside without even bothering
to answer her and Mrs. Treherne staggered backwards, her face white. Garnet was dragged bodily
from the hold and all her struggles availed her nothing
against the man's brute strength.

It was strange to be on deck with the sun warm on
her face and a soft breeze lifting her hair. She stared
out across the water but there was now no sign of the
Lady Elizabeth. She was taken to a large forecabin and
thrust unceremoniously inside.

The captain was dark and swarthy, and around his

neck was knotted a bright kerchief. His eyes glittered with malice as he looked her over from top to toe. In his hand was a knife that he tapped continuously on the table before him.

'I, Jose Sotelo.' The voice was soft, yet filled with menace. Garnet's heart sank, as any hope she'd harboured of appealing to the man's better nature vanished. He rose and walked slowly around the table. The blade of the knife was at her throat and a smile curved the captain's thin lips.

'The robe,' he said. 'Remove!' He allowed his eyes to fall to the softness of the curves beneath the gown she wore and, instinctively, Garnet drew away from him.

He caught a handful of her long hair and jerked her head back. Pain caused tears to rise to her eyes. With the blade, he cut through the thick material of her nightgown, revealing her white, uptilted breasts.

Garnet quickly drew the torn gown together, breathing heavily in distress. She had known he would be a scoundrel but this was something she could never have imagined in her wildest nightmares.

He tugged at her hair again and her neck arched back in agony as his hand reached inside the gown, catching her breast. Garnet pushed helplessly at his arm, her mouth dry, her heart beating rapidly.

The door opened suddenly and the captain released her, a scowl on his dark face. Garnet fell back against the wall trembling, thankful for the interruption.

The man who entered the cabin was tall and elegant. He was not a sailor, that much was apparent from the fine cut of his high-collared coat over the crisp shirt and blue silk vest. His breeches were of dark nankeen and his Hessian boots were well polished.

'Good morning, Captain Sotelo,' he said, and Garnet felt a rush of relief as she realized he was English. He glanced at her from under heavy lids. His eyes were grey, brooding, moving from her face to the shadow between her breasts. She drew her gown together quickly.

'Why you intrude, Señor Surbiton?' The captain was not pleased. His protuberant eyes darted from the man standing near the door to Garnet. 'You know each other?'

'No, we have never met.' The Englishman gave her a mocking bow. 'Perhaps, Captain, you could introduce us.'

Sotelo seemed confused. 'Your name, girl,' he said harshly.

'Garnet Kingdom.' She stared at the grey-eyed man who seemed so cool and composed, pleading silently for him to help her.

'Well, señor, you satisfied or is there other subject you would speak with me?'

'I would like to know when you will keep your side of our bargain and land me and my cargo at Tangiers.' His voice was low but brooked no argument.

'A day or so, señor, as soon as is possible. If that is all?'

The Englishman looked at Garnet again. 'She's quite a pretty little thing,' he said. 'Have you thought that you might get a good price for her in the slave market at Tangiers?'

The captain stared at Garnet with fresh appraisal and tapped his knife on the table for a few moments before answering.

'Could be so, señor,' he said at last.

Garnet stared at the two men in disbelief. They were calmly discussing the possibility of selling her as though she were a piece of furniture. She was aware of a keen sense of disappointment. When the Englishman had first entered the cabin and stared at her with his strange grey eyes, she had felt a glow of anticipation, hoping he was coming to her rescue, foolishly expecting him to act as a knight in shining armour. She had quickly been disillusioned.

'What is for you in this señor?' Captain Sotelo had returned to his seat behind the table. He was obviously suspicious. The Englishman shrugged lazily.

'I simply wish to arrive in Tangiers as soon as possible,' he said, turning towards the door. 'I believe I have given you good advice but, of course, you must do as you see fit with the girl.'

For a moment, his eyes seemed to look into Garnet's as though trying to convey some message, but then he was opening the door and his tall figure strode out into the sunshine of the deck.

The captain seemed to make up his mind abruptly. 'Manuel!' He called harshly and the huge sailor with the red bandanna on his coarse hair came striding on thick legs into the cabin.

'Take girl,' Sotelo gestured towards Garnet. 'See you lock her safely away. No one sees her, speaks with her. Understood?'

The man nodded and grasped Garnet's arm, drawing her outside into the brightness of the morning. He took her to a tiny cabin containing only a bunk and a small chest fastened against the wall. He thrust her inside and she heard the bolt being shot home.

She looked around her. There was no porthole and the only light was what penetrated the cracks in the door, but for all that, Garnet realized she was much more fortunate than the women who were still imprisoned in the airless hold.

She sank down onto the hard bunk and closed her eyes and saw again the handsome face of the man called Surbiton. Her heartbeats quickened as she remembered his heavily lidded eyes, dark grey, clear and penetrating. He was a fine-looking, handsome man and yet his lack of principles seemed equal to that of the Spanish captain. But he had mentioned Tangiers and there had been something in his parting glance that caused her to think even now that he might somehow manage to help her. She sighed, her feeling was probably nothing more than wishful thinking; she was looking for romance and she surely would not find it aboard the Spanish ship.

Later, Manuel brought her a tray of food. He placed it unceremoniously on the chest and stared at her with pebble black eyes.

'You eat,' he said. He would have left immediately but Garnet stopped him.

'Manuel,' she said softly. 'Who is this man Surbiton, why is he on board your ship?'

The Spaniard stared at her for a moment in silence

and then shrugged.

'What harm in telling you? He is Wolfe Surbiton, English gentleman.' He gave a thin smile. 'So he claims.'

'Do you doubt his word?' Garnet asked quickly and Manuel's grin vanished.

'He trades across seas in rum and cigars. It is said he will take any cargo, for a price.'

Garnet felt cold in spite of the heat. Upon such a man she had been pinning her hopes. It sounded as though he were little more than a pirate.

'We carry sugar cane for him now, and he pay well so Captain Sotelo accommodate him.' Manuel frowned. 'But he not be allowed interfere in our affairs.'

He shook his large head impatiently and left the tiny cabin, locking the door behind him.

So his name was 'Wolfe'. Garnet said it to herself and even though she knew she was being foolish, she imagined for a moment him rushing into the cabin, taking her in his arms and telling her he would protect her at whatever cost to himself.

Outside, there was silence except for the creak of the rigging and the crack as the wind filled the sails. Wolfe would not come. By now, probably, he would have completely forgotten her.

But Garnet was wrong. Wolfe Surbiton sat in his cabin, staring at the sun gleaming on the water outside. It was clear that he must form a plan to rescue the women. He could not allow Sotelo such brutality.

He smiled. He had given himself a breathing space,

and the young red-haired girl too. He had reckoned, and correctly, that Sotelo's greed would overcome his natural desire to hurt and crush any woman who caught his eye. The knife he played with continuously, the captain knew how to use, and with infinite cruelty.

Wolfe knew he would have to wait for nightfall before attempting to set the women free from the hold. He would ensure that a boat waited for them over the ship's side. Not even a bunch of women could lose their way so near to the coast. He would tell them to go to one of the British trading vessels in the harbour or to the English mission on the sea front. He would then be free of all feeling of responsibility for them and would be able to concentrate on his own plans and on getting his cargo safely to its destination.

He stretched his long legs before him, resting his Hessian boots on the small footstool. The girl, Garnet, she was a pretty little thing. Her eyes had turned to him with such appeal that he had felt compelled to think of a way of getting her out of Sotelo's clutches.

Careful, he warned himself. It was only too easy to be taken in by a pair of lovely eyes as he knew to his cost. He lay back and relaxed against the plump cushions on his chair. He might as well sleep away the heat of the day, for there was nothing he could do before darkness came.

Much later, he made his way below decks. He was searching for one of the Portuguese crewmen, knowing there was no love lost between them and their Spanish master. This was in his favour, making the matter of bribery very simple.

Soon, there was a boat bobbing on the silver seas and Wolfe crept silently towards the hatchway.

The women stared up at him from the dense blackness of the hold and he had to whisper to them urgently, before any of them would move.

Like ghosts, they drifted across the deck, climbing down the ladder into the boat below. One of them, her greying hair hanging down upon her shoulders, caught his hand and to his embarrassment kissed it.

'Go quickly,' he whispered. 'Head for one of the English ships. You will see their flags in the moonlight. Or go to the little mission near the tavern in the harbour.'

She nodded and clambered with difficulty over the rail, swaying a little as Wolfe helped her down the ladder.

Gamely, one of the women took up the oars and began to row and, as he leaned over the side, Wolfe strained his eyes, trying to see the tiny form of Garnet with her flowing red hair.

The craft was too crowded for him to pick her out and he felt a sense of dissatisfaction that she had not made an effort to thank him. He shrugged in the darkness and returned on light feet to his cabin. He should be well used to the ways of women by now. How many times did he have to be disillusioned before he learned that they all had sweet faces and treacherous hearts?

He had scarcely settled himself down in his bunk, when the door was flung open. Sotelo stood there, a lantern held aloft, his expression grim.

'The women, they have escaped,' he said harshly. He stared suspiciously at Wolfe who apparently had been asleep in his bunk.

'What is that to me?' Wolfe said sitting up and brushing back his hair with his hand. 'They are not my concern.'

Sotelo came further into the cabin. 'I think I believe you, señor,' he said more calmly. 'If it was you helped English ladies, the little red-haired wench would have gone also.' He smiled thinly. 'She still locked safely away. At least I make profit from selling her as you so kind suggested.'

Wolfe concealed the feeling of dismay the captain's words had given him.

'I sorry you been troubled, señor.' Sotelo retreated. 'Sleep well.'

Wolfe cursed himself for his stupidity. He might have known Sotelo would place the girl under a guard. The captain was not a fool. Wolfe's eyes were hard as they stared at the closed door of his cabin. He would not be thwarted. He would think of some other way of setting free the tiny English girl and, next time, he would not fail.

CHAPTER TWO

The heat was intolerable as was the stench of un-
washed bodies. Clouds of flies swarmed around
Garnet, who stood bound hand and foot in the hot
sand of Tangiers. She stared along the silver ark of the
bay to where the Spanish ship lay at anchor in the
azure sea. Her spirits rose a little; at least the other
women had escaped from Sotelo's cruelty and now
Caroline would meet her lover after all.

From the luminous edge of the water, a chain of
men, tall and black, passed bales of cotton from hand
to hand. A gigantic native lifted a cask of rum with
ease and carried it through the stinging white sand on
his gleaming shoulder.

'Come, we move now.' Manuel had been refreshing
himself from an earthenware jug of rum. He mopped
his sweating forehead with a grubby kerchief and
tugged at the chains that bound her.

Listlessly, Garnet began to walk, anything would be
better than standing under the merciless sun. At first,
in the early hours of sunlight, before Manuel had
brought her ashore, Garnet had hoped that she too

might be rescued. Gradually as the day wore on, she had become resigned to the fact that Wolfe would not come for her.

Soon, they came to the town of Tangiers itself. Garnet stared up at the sunbaked walls closing in on her and, for a moment, she felt she could not breathe. She faltered and Manuel growled his disapproval.

'You, red one, keep moving.' His thick legs plodded forward sending up spurts of dust around his sandalled feet. Garnet shook her head, trying to clear her mind.

The alleyway opened out into a small square and the noise of many people speaking in a strange language was almost like a blow. Men heavily robed, in spite of the heat, sat cross-legged on colourful mats, an array of merchandise set out before them. Delicate copper ornaments gleamed in the dust beside finely worked leather knife-holders.

Manuel bent his great bulk, the silk of his pantaloons straining at the seams. He picked up a piece of plaited leather and held it against Garnet's thighs.

'You look good in a haggu,' he said, and the man seated on the floor laughed loudly. Encouraged, Manuel held the strip closer to Garnet's body.

'You know what it is, red one? A loincloth for black wenches. You wear it for me?'

Garnet stared at him in contempt; she knew that to show fear was to place herself in Manuel's power.

'Your captain would cut off your ears if he could see you now,' she said fiercely. Manuel looked round quickly, as though he feared Jose Sotelo himself might appear at his side.

'We go.' He spoke in a surly voice. 'We waste time.' He jerked cruelly on the chains and Garnet was pulled forward.

A small girl with a basket over her arm stopped to stare at the white woman. Garnet smelled the sharp, mouthwatering scent of lemons and a wave of homesickness washed over her. She closed her eyes, imagining herself at home, on the terrace, sipping cordial.

She stumbled over a sack of highly coloured spices, almost falling to her knees. Lining the roadway were women crouched beside huge baskets of flowers. Dark eyes, above heavy face veils, stared at her with curiosity.

As she followed Manuel through yet another net-work of narrow alleyways, Garnet's lips were dry, her throat aching with the heat and dust.

'I must rest.' She leaned against the warmth of one of the walls, hardly able to breathe. Manuel stared at her suspiciously for a moment and then shrugged. He slipped the goat-skin water bag from his shoulder. 'Drink only little,' he spoke ungraciously, but Garnet was already tasting the water, sweet and fresh against her lips. She tipped a little of the sparkling liquid onto her hands, pressing her fingers to the scorched and burned skin of her face.

'Enough of resting.' Manuel was impatient to be moving. 'Give me the girby.' He placed the bag on his shoulder and began to walk. Garnet hurried after him, not wishing to feel the bite of the steel chains against her flesh. Her wrists and ankles were badly cut and she realized that Manuel was a mindless creature who did not understand that his unthinking cruelty was making the journey more difficult.

It was a relief to reach the large market place on the outskirts of Tangiers. Green fronded palm trees waved against the clear sky, blocking the sun's rays so that the air was cooler. When Manuel came to a halt, Garnet fell to her knees, head bowed, hair hanging in the dust.

Manuel unlocked the chains. 'No try to run,' he said thickly. His face was grim, sweat ran into the creases of his brow. 'Nowhere to go, understand?' he insisted.

Garnet nodded, unable to speak. She would not have the strength to run, even if she wanted to. She lifted her head and saw a wide dais of wood in the centre of the market. This then was where slaves were bought and sold. Soon, she would be one of them.

A horn sounded mournfully on the hot afternoon air and, at her side, Manuel lifted his great head to stare across the clearing. Following the direction of his gaze, Garnet saw a young dark-skinned girl being dragged forward. She wore a clean white shift and a turban of yellow cloth covered her head. She twisted in terror, trying to free herself from the hands of her captor, but her struggles were in vain. Her arms were twisted behind her back and, with one movement, the shift was torn from her slender body. The girl gave a thin scream, her dark eyes were wide with fear as robed men gathered round to stare at her nakedness. Garnet felt shame and anger burn within her, knowing that she too would be put on the block, subjected to the same humiliation.

The bidding was quickly over and Manuel heaved himself to his feet, grasping Garnet's arm in a grip of steel.

'We go next.' He drew her after him, careless of the fact that she was tripping over the hem of her robe. He stood her in the centre of the platform and spoke in what Garnet guessed was halting Arabic.

She was acutely conscious of the robed men staring in curiosity but she held herself upright, struggling to prevent the tears from spilling down her hot cheeks. A harsh voice rang out, speaking words Garnet could not understand, and Manuel caught her robe, tearing the soft silk easily with his great fingers. When she attempted to draw the tattered garment around her body, he twisted her arm behind her back with fierce anger.

The bidding began in earnest and voices rang out around her. Manuel's smile broadened and his huge head swung from side to side as he tried to keep count of the offers being made for the white girl with the flame-coloured hair.

Finally, one of the men mounted the dais. He lifted her head and his hands were rough on her cheeks, examining her with keen scrutiny. He forced her lips apart and looked at her teeth and then his hands were running along her body, feeling the weight of her breasts, the curve of her hips, but all with lack of emotion as though he was purchasing a piece of furniture.

He nodded and handed a pouch of money to Manuel who smiled gleefully.

'Good-bye, red one. I hope your new master teach you obedience with a whip.'

Garnet was thrust from the dais and immediately a woman came forward holding a coarse white robe, eyes downcast. Garnet took it with shaking hands, drawing it around her, tying the waist securely with the tasselled belt.

Behind her, the sale of human flesh was still taking place. Garnet closed her eyes in despair. She was no longer her own mistress, she had been bought and paid for, she was nothing more than a possession.

The woman, eyes still downcast, touched Garnet's arm and silently led her away from the heat and noise of the market place, through an arched doorway into a mellow biscuit-coloured building. She was ushered into a high-ceilinged room filled with brilliant silk cushions and left alone.

Garnet sighed, she was weary and dispirited and it hardly seemed to matter what became of her. Nevertheless, when the ornate gilt handle on the door began to turn, she withdrew against the drapes of the wall, her heart beating swiftly.

'Wolfe!' Garnet blinked rapidly, unable to believe her eyes. He stood before her, smiling lazily, appearing amazingly cool, his shirt crisp and clean, his Hessian boots gleaming with polish.

Her first instinct was to run into the safety of his arms and cling to him, but then a cold anger grew within her. Had he come sooner she would have been saved the humiliation of being sold as a slave.

'You are too late,' she said flatly. To her surprise, he gave a short laugh.

'I have been bought by a stranger. He now owns me.' Garnet could not keep the bitterness from her voice. Wolfe drew nearer, placing his hands on her shoulders.

'I own you,' he said easily. 'I used an agent to bargain on my behalf. You're my property, Garnet.'

She stared up at him in silence. How could he have allowed her to endure the public humiliation of being put on the block? She recoiled from him and his smile vanished.

'I do not intend to ravish you but I do intend to make a reasonable profit when I return you to your father,' he said curtly.

'Never fear.' Garnet's voice was harsh. 'My father is a man of honour; he will pay his debt to you.'

'I'm pleased to hear it,' Wolfe said. 'But unfortunately, it will be some time before I can put your words to the test.'

Garnet looked at him. 'What do you mean?' He wandered around the room, picking up a small figurine, studying it as though he had nothing better to do with his time.

'I have business here in North Africa,' he said. 'It is time you realized I'm not here solely for your benefit.'

Garnet bit her lip, wondering if she could persuade Wolfe to take her to the British brig in Tangiers harbour. She stared at his set face and the strong line of his jaw and knew there was no hope of diverting him from the plans he had already made.

A servant entered, carrying a dish of rice and a large platter filled with slices of mutton. She bowed to Wolfe, offering him food.

When she had bowed her way backwards from the room, Wolfe turned to Garnet.

'You had better eat something,' he said abruptly. 'I mean to set out within the hour. You can ride a horse, I hope.'

'Yes.' Garnet could not take her eyes away from the dish of steaming juicy meat. She had not realized how hungry she was.

It tasted as delicious as it looked, with a tantalizing aroma of strange herbs meant to stimulate the appetite. Garnet sank onto one of the cushions taking another slice of meat between her fingers. She heard Wolfe laugh.

'You take to native ways very quickly,' he said. 'And that's just as well, there's precious little comfort where we're going.'

'What do you mean?' Garnet asked quickly, but Wolfe had turned away from her as though he'd failed to hear her question. He looked so handsome, his hair curling on his brow, his eyes hidden from her by dark lashes, that Garnet's heart missed a beat. He turned slowly as though aware of her scrutiny and they stared at each other without speaking. Wolfe broke the spell by thrusting his hands into his pockets and moving towards the door.

'We shall have to be leaving here shortly.' His voice sounded strange. 'There have been enough delays.'

He strode out of the building and Garnet was forced to run after him into the sunlit square. Wolfe was already untethering a fine black stallion, leading the graceful creature from the shade of the palm tree into the clearing at the front of the house. A flat wooden saddle was strapped to the horse's shining flanks along with two great girbies of water and a bulging saddlebag.

'I hope you can ride reasonably well,' he said without looking at her. 'Otherwise you'll have a very long walk.' There was no glimmer of a smile on his face and Garnet was hurt by his careless attitude.

'I can ride perfectly well,' she said in a small cold voice. He turned and lifted her into the saddle, swinging himself up behind her, his arm warm against her waist. His hands shook the reins and the horse moved forward.

As the town of Tangiers was left behind, Garnet found herself relaxing against his broad shoulder. A feeling of happiness was stealing over her as she breathed in his masculine scent.

The horse was moving more slowly now, under the evening sun that bounced heat up from the fine sand. Garnet was half asleep, imagining that she and Wolfe were setting off on an adventure together from choice. She wished to forget that he had taken the trouble to buy her simply so that he might make a profit when he returned her to her father.

In the circle of his arms, she felt safe and cherished. His cheek was resting against her hair, almost tenderly. But the illusion of closeness vanished as soon as he spoke.

'We'd better rest a moment.' He slid down from the horse and looked up at her with grey, impersonal eyes. 'I shall need to water the animal so stretch your legs if you like.'

He set her on the softly moving sand and released her at once, lifting one of the heavy girbies from the saddle and turning his attention to the horse who, smelling water, whinnied softly.

Garnet sank down onto her knees. She was, quite suddenly, unbearably sleepy. It might have been the glare of the sunlight stretching across the endless ripples of sand that forced her to close her eyes. She heard the droning of some desert creature on the still air and she slept.

It was Wolfe's touch on her arm that woke her; she stared upwards, not knowing for a moment where she was. She was lying in the circle of his arms and he was looking at her with a steady unwavering regard that brought the colour to her cheeks. She would have moved away, but he held her fast. His fingers strayed from her arm to the opening of her robe and found her breast. She gasped.

'Please don't.' Her voice was little more than a whisper. Sensations were racing through her blood, feelings she'd never known before, and her arms reached up and caught his neck, drawing his mouth towards hers.

When he kissed her, it was as though the world had dissolved into a hundred tiny fragments. The sun was blotted out of the sky.

He lifted his head and smiled down at her. 'It is

strange how attractive a woman becomes when she is the only one for miles around.' he said lazily. He moved away from her, brushing the sand from his clothes, unaware of the turmoil of emotions he had aroused in Garnet's heart.

'Come along,' he said, staring across the bright golden peaks and deep shadows of the sand dunes. 'We have a lot of ground to make up if we are to reach our destination before nightfall.'

Garnet was too bewildered by her own feelings to do anything but obey him. He was cold and callous and yet she had been so contented lying in his arms. Even when he had touched her breasts, it had seemed beautiful and right, as though they belonged together, she and Wolfe. But he had only been amusing himself. It seemed impossible to believe that the magic of the moment had left him untouched. His lips had been warm on hers, taking possession of her, and then, deliberately, he had shattered the illusion.

The sun began to go down over the horizon, a large orb of red and gold, washing the sand with colours of amber and jet. The shadows were deep and stark and the horse stepped uneasily into them, ears high.

'We should not have delayed so long.' Wolfe spoke impatiently, as though Garnet were to blame for falling asleep. She sighed, pushing herself away from his shoulder, and as she did so, the animal stumbled. Garnet felt herself flung forward. She rolled in the sand, the breath knocked from her body. She stared up in panic to see Wolfe outlined against the night sky, his head bent over the fallen horse.

After a few moments, he reached into the saddle bag. Garnet saw his silhouette against the night sky, his arm outstretched, holding a pistol. She closed her eyes as the shot resounded in the silence, her hands covering her face.

'We are going to walk, do you understand?' He lifted her bodily to her feet, his hands under her arms. 'There is nothing to fear, I know this desert well.'

She glanced towards the dark huddled shape of the stallion and Wolfe shook his head.

'A broken leg,' he said briefly. 'Come along.' He shouldered the girby and began to stride ahead. Garnet followed him though the difficulties of their situation seemed insurmountable. She felt like striking out at Wolfe as though he were responsible for all her misfortunes. Sand chafed her cut ankles but she was determined not to complain. It was almost dark by now with the wind cool and the sky overcast. She was moving through instinct alone and she knew she could not go on much further.

Almost senseless, she felt Wolfe swing her into his arms. The crispness of his shirt was beneath her cheek and she felt his heart beating as though it were her own. She imagined he kissed her brow, but that was nonsense because Wolfe Surbiton was a man completely devoid of tenderness.

Wolfe was making steady progress in spite of the heaviness of the powdery sand that sucked at his boots. The moon was a silver crescent now, making a snowy landscape that was illusory but beautiful.

Garnet was a sweet burden in his arms and, as Wolfe looked down into her sleeping face, he was tempted to kiss her slightly parted lips. She was beautiful in the moonlight, her lashes dark fans against the pale of her skin. The white column of her throat led his eyes to the intriguing shadows between her breasts. He stumbled and, cursing, forced himself to look ahead. He did not need his compass to tell him the direction he must take, he had travelled the same route at least a hundred times in the last four years, ever since he had formed a partnership with Jonathon Summers.

The desert was constantly changing, the sand restless and shifting, but Wolfe had found his own signs in the stunted trees and curiously shaped rocks. He knew he must be drawing close to the ancient, isolated mosque where he had sheltered on several occasions from the cold of the desert nights.

The wind was rising and the sand stung his face like the assault of a myriad insects. It was a relief to see the walls of the old building rising black against the moonlight. He stepped down into the intense blackness of the interior and carefully laid Garnet down against the cave-like wall. As his eyes became accustomed to the gloom, he found his way to the stone shelf where a lantern stood and, as he lit the candle, a warm glow flickered against the roof.

He crouched on the ground, drawing off his Hessians; he leaned back against the wall and took a drink from the girby. Tonight he had only water but tomorrow he would drink sweet rum. One thing he could say for Summers, he knew how to produce the best liquor and the finest cigars in the whole of Africa.

It was a strange partnership, Wolfe mused, between himself and Summers, the fifty-year-old white man who had gone native. They had met in a run-down bar in Tangiers, and when Wolfe had succumbed to the raw native wine, Summers had removed him to his low, rambling house on the edge of the desert. Wolfe had recovered from his bout of drinking to find Summers operating an illegal still, bringing sugar cane in small quantities from the West Indies and supplying most of the ships that docked in Tangiers with the matured rum. Seeing the potential in the business, Wolfe had invested his money in new equipment and now, four years later, was reaping his reward. While not a rich man, he was at least comfortably placed. Only once had Summers questioned him about his past and Wolfe's reaction had convinced him it was wiser to mind his own business.

Garnet stirred, sighing a little in her sleep, and Wolfe turned to look at her. She was completely relaxed, her limbs spread on the sandy floor, her hair flowing around her white shoulders. She was a lovely creature and so different to Lucia. He pulled himself up sharply. What made him think of her at this moment? Perhaps it was his memories of meeting Jonathon Summers that brought her to mind. Lucia had been the reason for his immoderate drinking, she had the face of a madonna and the heart of a witch. She had given him the sweetness of her lovely body and then spurned him, telling him flatly that he would never match up to her adoring papa's idea of a perfect husband.

He rose to his feet and walked to the doorway, staring out into the darkness. At least Lucia had taught him one thing and that was never to trust a pretty face and a pair of innocent eyes.

He forced his thoughts away from the painful memories. Tomorrow, he would press on to the home of his partner. They would sit on the veranda and watch the sunset, talking about the business with an easy friendship. This was the world in which Wolfe was sure of himself; it gave him great satisfaction to flout authority, making money beneath the noses of the English sailors.

From time to time there were raids on the property of Jonathon Summers, but the man was highly organized by now. He could remove incriminating evidence in a very short time and all that would be found was a warehouse full of cigars imported legitimately from Havana. But then Summers was careful enough to have one of his men working aboard the English vessel and was always alerted of impending visits.

Wolfe himself supplied the perfect front, the son of an English lord and a Spanish countess, he had an air of respectability that was unassailable. That his parents' death had left him with a mass of debts was no one's concern but his own.

He sighed deeply, staring out into the night; such introspection was no good, it was time he got some sleep. He lay down beside Garnet, drawing a strange sensation of pleasure from her nearness. He smiled to himself in the darkness. What he was experiencing was simply the natural urge of a man for a woman, nothing more.

CHAPTER THREE

Garnet was the first one to see the line of men in war-paint, spears and shields at the ready, staring down from the brow of the hill. It was less than an hour since Wolfe had woken her from sleep, telling her coldly that it was time they started out before the sun became too hot. At first, as she saw the movement on the ridge, she thought her weary eyes were playing her false but as she drew nearer to the greener slope of the highlands her worst fears were confirmed.

'We're being watched,' she said to Wolfe who was a little way ahead of her. He did not stop walking but glanced casually to the rise, his eyes narrowed against the glare of the sky.

Even as Garnet watched, the line dissolved and the men were plunging down the hill with fierce cries that struck terror to her heart. She hurried towards Wolfe and was surprised to see him smiling.

'There's nothing to fear,' he said. 'These are old friends of mine.' He was quickly surrounded and the men were almost as tall as he was. Dark skin glistened in the sunlight under brilliant markings from cheek bone to jaw. Garnet fell back a step, still frightened in spite of Wolfe's reassurance.

'You must kneel and touch your forehead to the ground,' Wolfe said to her, and when she stared at him in surprise, his tone hardened. 'At once.'

Awkwardly, she knelt, her head against the dry, sandy earth. She felt Wolfe's hand on her shoulder and the pressure of his fingers warned her to remain where she was. Dimly, she realized that this gesture of sub-servience must be a tribal custom. Obediently, she waited until his hand was under her arm, lifting her to her feet.

'These are the men of the Bagger tribe,' he ex-plained. 'They seem very impressed with your beauty.' His hand slipped to her waist. 'They believe you are my woman,' he smiled. 'I'd better warn you that it's best to allow them to go on thinking that, otherwise I might have to offend one of them by refus-ing to barter you for a sack of salt or a few jars of oil.'

One of the men lifted a lock of Garnet's hair, twist-ing and turning it in the sun, apparently fascinated by the gleaming colour.

'We are invited to their village,' Wolfe continued. 'It would be ill mannered of me to refuse though in truth I cannot spare the time. But, we shall have to make the best of it. You must remember to walk behind me, is that understood?'

Garnet nodded, refraining from pointing out that it was his usual practice to stride on ahead of her and that she was well used to seeing his broad back.

The desert was slowly giving way to a terrain richer

in foliage. Strong trees reached up towards bright clear skies and amid the sandy soil grew sturdy grasses, coarse and yellow.

The village appeared to be well hidden among the rocks but at last it came into view. Domed huts made of mud sprang like mushrooms from the ground, light grey in colour, doors covered with bright rugs.

In the clearing sat the women of the tribe, and on the arrival of their menfolk, they immediately prostrated themselves upon the ground.

The tribe leader moved among the women, speaking with quiet authority. Garnet saw them look up, laughing like children, and one of the women pointed to where Garnet stood beside Wolfe.

'It seems we are to be given a feast of welcome,' he said, glancing towards Garnet. 'They wish to celebrate our union.'

She knew he was amused by the situation. She deliberately avoided his eyes, staring down at her clenched hands. He couldn't have made his feelings more obvious, she meant less than nothing to him and she wondered why the thought was so painful.

A dark-skinned girl stood before her, speaking softly, head on one side. Garnet stared at her helplessly and it was Wolfe who came to her aid.

'She is telling you that her name is Ajaj,' he explained. 'She wishes you to go with her to the long hut of the spirit of the earth.'

Garnet followed the lithe figure of Ajaj to the very edge of the village and saw that the long hut was well named. It was a low mud building with no windows and only a small door so that Garnet was forced to bend her head to enter. The interior was lit with a shell of oil bearing a tallow and the flame flickered eerily in the dimness.

Ajaj brought a bowl of water and a soft scent like that of wild roses drifted from the surface. Garnet understood, from the dark girl's gestures, that she should wash.

The dusty robe fell in folds around her feet and Garnet was shyly aware of Ajaj's curiosity as she stared at the marble-white skin. She nodded and left Garnet alone and it was good to feel the soft scented water washing away the sand from her body.

The dark girl returned after only a few minutes carrying a gown of rich blue silk decorated with crystal beads and tiny seed pearls. Ajaj bowed to Garnet, presenting the garment with a flourish and insisting with high, excited speech and eager gestures on helping Garnet to dress.

When she returned to the clearing, Garnet was aware of Wolfe's eyes taking in every detail of her appearance. The fine silk clung to the curves of her body and the lustre of the gown complimented the red gold of her hair.

He too had been subjected to the ministrations of the tribeswomen. He stood tall and breathtakingly handsome, garbed in a white robe that flowed from his broad shoulders to the ground.

Ajaj urged Garnet forward and she saw that she was to sit at Wolfe's feet. He smiled down at her and she bit her lip, knowing he was enjoying her humiliation. He touched her shoulder, his fingers caressing, warm through the thin silk. She met his eyes and for a long breathless moment they stared in silence at each other. His smile had vanished and he seemed to be searching for something in her face. Abruptly, he turned away, talking to the tribe leader in his own language, and it was as though the moment had been merely a figment of her imagination.

The silk of her robe shimmered before her eyes and she was impatient with herself. Wolfe had made it plain there was nothing between them and, for her part, why on earth should she care what he thought of her? Theirs was simply a business relationship and that was just the way she wanted it.

The men seemed to talk endlessly and the heat of the day turned to indigo. Garnet found her position at Wolfe's feet uncomfortable and cramped. Ajaj had busied herself weaving a necklace of oleander flowers and when it was finished, she slipped it over Garnet's head with a smile.

From the far end of the clearing, a fire roared and crackled, sending sparks of light up into the night sky. The smell of roasting meat made Garnet aware of how hungry she was. She glanced up at Wolfe who was being handed a platter and shrank back instinctively as she saw the head of a ram, complete with horns and eyes, steaming from the heat of the fire.

Wolfe merely pinched a piece of the meat between his thumb and forefinger, eating it with apparent relish. He smiled at her and leaned forward.

'Try not to wear such a look of disgust, Garnet, this

is a great delicacy intended only for the men.'

Ajaj gave her a bowl of rice, nodding encouragement. The grain was yellowish but edible and, as Garnet ate, a wing of capon was added to the rice along with a handful of peppers.

The food was delicious and Garnet was aware of Ajaj's approving look as she emptied the bowl.

Cups of dark thick liquid were passed around and Garnet stared down at it suspiciously.

'It's merely rum and nut oil,' Wolfe said in amusement. 'It really won't hurt you. Take it, you'll need it to wash down the cassava roots which are our next course.'

Garnet saw what Wolfe meant when she tried to eat the tough, stringy plant that tasted like raw, hot pepper. She was grateful to Ajaj for refilling her cup and drank deeply, trying not to cough.

Garnet felt herself sway, the ground seemed to undulate before her eyes and she found herself laughing helplessly as she gave up all attempts to finish the meal. She felt Wolfe's hand on her arm.

'Be careful, Garnet, the local brew is sweet but it has a sting. You're drinking it far too quickly.'

She opened her mouth to make a retort but he caught her in his arms, his mouth close to her ear.

'Don't answer me back,' he whispered. 'Otherwise it will appear that you have lost favour with me.'

Garnet was breathlessly aware of his nearness, she forced herself to speak coherently.

'Does it matter what these people think?' she whispered back, trying to untangle herself from his arms.

'I'm sure it does,' Wolfe leaned away from her, smiling down into her eyes, keeping his voice low. 'I should probably be offered a young virgin in your place which I imagine I might find very pleasant.'

'Why not accept then?' she said and, though she meant to sound defiant, her voice was shaking and strangely unconvincing.

'I don't think you would like the reciprocal gesture I would be forced to make,' he said, kissing her lips lightly.

'I don't understand.' Garnet's heart was beating swiftly, she was staring into his eyes, resisting the longing to wind her arms around his neck and return his kiss.

'I should be obliged to offer you to the tribal chief for the night,' he said dryly. 'It would only be neighbourly.'

She digested his words in silence, trying to make sense of them. Did Wolfe mean that, as things stood, she and he were to share the same bed, and if she protested, she would be taken by the chief?

Wolfe released her. 'I see you understand the situation,' he said lightly. 'I trust you will find the experience of sleeping with me not without its compensations.'

She looked away from him; she was still not sure if he was serious or simply making fun of her. With a man like Wolfe, it was not easy to read his thoughts.

Unthinkingly, she drank from her cup once more, her mind in a turmoil. Wolfe might feel she was ready to fall into his arms, he had such a high opinion of his charm. But he would find she was not at all moved by him, even though the tribeswomen were staring at him as though he was some wonderful god.

Garnet felt a sharp sting on the bare flesh of her arm. She saw a winged creature dark against her white skin and brushed it away quickly.

'Mosquitoes,' Wolfe said. 'They thrive in the damp regions surrounding the river. It will be better once we go to bed.'

He was teasing her this time, Garnet was sure, and she turned away from him. He spoke to the chief in his own language and the man laughed, resting his hand for a moment on the silk of Garnet's hair, almost as though he were blessing her.

'What is the man saying?' Garnet asked Wolfe anxiously and he smiled.

'It's a good thing I've broken bread with the tribe so often,' he said. 'The chief finds you very lovely, he would have taken you away to his bed by now if he hadn't believed you were my woman.'

Garnet lifted her cup and drank with complete disregard for Wolfe's warning. She knew that she was affected by the rum but the closeness of Wolfe's hand resting on her shoulder, almost touching her breast, disturbed her more.

The fire was dying low and the sky was a vast, indigo bowl encrusted with stars when at last Wolfe rose to his feet, bowing slowly to the chief.

'Come Garnet, it is time for us to retire,' he said, and she stepped forward hesitantly, glad of Ajaj's supporting arm around her waist.

A group of young maidens walked with Garnet towards the long hut where Garnet had been taken earlier. What was the name they gave it? The spirit of the earth, that was it. Garnet stared at the candle inside the doorway and the light wavered unsteadily before her eyes.

Ajaj guided her towards a rear chamber, holding the candle high. It was the strangest room Garnet had ever seen, the walls were lined with green trailing weed that smelled vaguely like thyme. On the floor was a wide pallet covered in bright cotton blankets.

Wolfe appeared at Garnet's side. 'The ladies intend to see us safely to bed,' he said. 'It is their usual practice to wait until their guests are settled for the night before sealing up the doorway with the greenery, their method for keeping out mosquitoes. It seems, Garnet, that we shall pass the night in some degree of comfort.'

Ajaj was bowing before Wolfe, calling the other girls forward and, with quick looks from beneath dark lashes, they began to help him disrobe. Garnet quickly averted her eyes from his long, tanned body. Her colour rose as Ajaj smiled and held out her hands for Garnet's silk gown.

Quickly, she climbed beneath the sheets, leaving as much space as possible between herself and Wolfe. Ajaj giggled and, with a bow, withdrew and Garnet saw the hanging of weed placed over the doorway.

'We can't sleep together like this,' Garnet said breathlessly, her heart beating unusually fast. She felt his hand touch her arm and she longed to move closer, to be held in the safety of his arms.

'I don't see that there is any alternative,' Wolfe said. 'If you move out of this room, you are liable to be eaten alive by mosquitoes.'

'I thought you might sleep in the other chamber,' Garnet said, and even as she spoke she realized she might as well be asking for the moon. He gave a short laugh.

'No thanks, I'm quite happy where I am.' His thigh accidentally touched hers and Garnet closed her eyes tightly, fighting the rush of emotions that swept over her. She should not have drunk so freely of the rum and nut oil; it was affecting her in the strangest way. Her heart was racing and her mind seemed unable to function properly.

'Oh, why don't you go away and leave me alone?' she said in a small desperate voice, her bewilderment at her own feelings making her impatient.

Wolfe leaned over her in sudden anger. He gripped her arms tightly, his eyes gleaming in the eerie green light. He looked strangely unreal, his bare shoulder warm as she reached out a hand to push him away.

There was a long silence and then, slowly, they came together, and afterwards, she was never sure who it was made the first move. His mouth was touching hers, lightly at first and then with deepening passion, and her fingers caressed the smooth skin of his arm. She was lost in a sensation of happiness, a feeling that all that was happening to her now was meant to be.

The long length of him was close to her as they lay

thigh to thigh. His hand moved from the hollow of her waist, to cup her breast, his fingers gently teasing the nipple. She drew a ragged breath, knowing that she should stop him now before it was too late. But she lacked the strength to push him away, she wanted his touch, wanted the wonderful feeling of joy to continue.

His hand moved down her hip, as though tracing the shape of her body. He was still kissing her, his tongue probing hers, and she was clinging to him as though she would never let him go.

His fingers touched her thighs, finding the secrets of her flesh, moving gently and yet with a sureness that sent flames of desire racing through her. It was already too late to draw back. Whatever the consequences, she must learn all that Wolfe had to teach.

He rose above her slowly and for a moment she felt a sense of panic as she saw how strong and large he was. He kissed her breasts so tenderly that tears sprang to her eyes.

Slowly, he moved downwards, penetrating her receptive softness. She knew pain and she cried out but he captured her mouth with his, silencing her, and she trusted him. He continued to move carefully, making gentle progress, and the pain was overcome by a wave of passion so fierce that she began to move too, lifting herself against him. She longed to urge him to greater efforts but she was afraid and shy. She clung to his shoulders and he seemed to sense what she wanted and his thrusts became stronger, quicker, taking utter possession of her until it seemed that her mind and soul were his as well as her body.

The final shuddering ecstasy was so intense that Garnet arched backwards, moaning softly. The sensation seemed to continue as Wolfe too reached the heights, holding her as tightly as he could, giving her the sensation of being moulded into his body, truly one with him.

When it was over, Wolfe held her cradled in his arms, her head in the warm hollow of his shoulder. Garnet knew she had crossed a threshold and could never return to the innocent she had been before this night. She drifted off to sleep with a feeling of happiness around her like a blanket, safe in the warmth of Wolfe's arms.

She was awake before Wolfe and, in his sleep, he had moved away from her, to the other side of the pallet. She leaned on her elbow, looking down at the smooth strong lines of his face and the dark sweep of his lashes against his cheeks. She shivered as she remembered lying in his arms, giving herself to him unreservedly. The happiness had been almost too much to bear and yet now she wondered what he must be thinking of her. She had given her love so readily in almost wanton abandonment.

His eyes opened suddenly and Garnet felt the colour rise to her cheeks. She smiled at him uncertainly, hoping he would take her in his arms and tell her of his love. But without speaking, he rose from the sheets, striding across the room and flinging down the covering of weeds that barred his way to the outer chamber. She heard the splash of water and knew that he was not going to return to her. She hugged herself, closing her eyes, longing for him to tell her that what happened between them was wonderful and precious.

Ajaj entered the hut and Garnet saw her bow to Wolfe before handing him his freshly laundered clothes. She disappeared to return within a few minutes carrying a bowl which she placed beside Garnet. She smiled and the scent of flowers hung heavily in the air.

Garnet completed her simple toilet with Ajaj standing near, holding a fresh gown of brightly patterned cotton over her brown arm. Nothing seemed real, it was as though the events of the night had been a dream and yet Garnet recalled so vividly the feelings Wolfe had awoken in her.

Ajaj took Garnet's arm, leading her out into the warmth of the early morning. The acacia trees swayed in the dry breeze, thorns gleaming with moisture like tears.

Wolfe was eating breakfast. A young girl knelt before him holding a platter of fish rolled in green leaves, her dark eyes adoring. Garnet crouched beside him on the colourful mat and he glanced at her briefly.

Ajaj offered Garnet a bowl of fruit and her eyes were sad as though she sensed all was not well.

'Have a good breakfast,' Wolfe said coolly. 'We shall be travelling for most of the day and I do not wish to stop again.'

Garnet picked at the raisins but every mouthful felt as though it might choke her. She knew she would have to speak to him, try to break through the barrier he had raised between them.

'Wolfe, what's wrong, are you disappointed in me? Please don't treat me as though I was a stranger.'

He might not have heard. He continued to eat without looking at her and Ajaj placed more food beside Garnet who shook her head.

The girl finally withdrew, taking with her the remains of the meal. Wolfe rose to his feet, dressed once more in his crisp shirt, freshly washed for him, and his Hessians, shined and polished until he could see his face in them.

'You might as well understand one thing,' he said, his hands resting on his hips, his eyes staring out across the dry dusty land. 'Last night meant nothing at all, is that clear?'

Garnet felt her heart sink; for a moment she thought she might be sick. She drew herself up and forced herself to speak calmly.

'Of course I understand.' She was surprised at her own control. 'It meant nothing to either of us, it was simply a pleasant interlude, one that won't be repeated.'

She watched as he strode away from her and her fingers were clenched so hard into fists that her nails cut into her flesh. She had been a foolish innocent to believe that Wolfe Surbiton might be in love with her. It seemed that a man of his sort took a woman as he ate a meal, for temporary gratification. He had taught her a lesson and she meant to learn it well, that trust and love were merely words, they meant nothing more than the dust beneath Wolfe's feet.

CHAPTER FOUR

Wolfe was happy to leave his friends, the Bagger tribesmen, behind. Kind they might be but they had forced him into a closeness with Garnet that he did not welcome. She had been sweet and responsive in his arms, her eyes soft as he made love to her, but women were so good at setting traps and he had no intention of being caught again.

Their progress was slow. The chief had no horses but had given Wolfe the next best thing, a stubborn old donkey, an animal unused to long journeys. Garnet sat uncomfortably on the creature's back, her mouth set as though she was determined not to complain.

He found himself wondering about her. He had expected a cloying, emotional scene from her this morning but she had surprised him with her attitude of indifference. He was more than a little peeved by her casual observation that the intimacy between them would not be repeated.

At the time, it had delighted him to learn that she was a virgin. There was something satisfying about being the first with a woman, any woman. But later, he had lain awake in the darkness, troubled that Garnet would take his natural urges as an expression of undying love.

Lucia had experienced several lovers before him. The dark, Spanish beauty who looked so cool on the surface was a cauldron of seething emotion, making demands upon a man, twisting him to her own advantage. He still grew angry when he remembered how she had discarded him, no doubt for a new lover. And all the while, her unsuspecting father believed she was so untouched and innocent.

His anger was revealed in the way he strode rapidly over the yellow grass, dragging at the reins of the reluctant donkey. He could see in the distance the high, baked rocks that surrounded the home of his partner, Jonathon Summers, and Wolfe sighed with relief. Soon the uncomfortable journey would be over and he would be free of Garnet's silent presence.

'Almost there,' he said flatly, and she met his eyes, her gaze unwavering. She had borne the heat with a stoicism that had earned his respect. Her hair hung in damp strands across her face, her skin reddened by the sun, and still she was beautiful.

The small huddle of buildings were in sight now, casting deep long shadows onto the courtyard. Acacia trees surrounded the main house, thorny fingers pointing towards the sun. It was difficult to believe that the sea was less than a mile away to the north.

He could picture Summers sitting on the veranda, sipping a long glass of lemon cordial liberally laced with gin. He would be wearing faded breeches and an old patched shirt as he always did. No one would suspect by his appearance that Summers was now a wealthy man.

That he had many concubines among the native women from the nearby village was common knowledge. Beautiful women they were too, long of limb and golden brown with large dark eyes. And yet Wolfe had never been tempted to follow his partner's example, but then Esther was always there at the house, waiting patiently for him. Summers' offspring were easy to recognize, Wolfe thought dryly. The children invariably inherited his straight flaxen hair.

On reaching adulthood, a select few of his daughters would be sent into the hills to be trained as warriors. Only the strongest and tallest would be chosen, the perfect ones, with straight regular features.

Jonathon had confided once that he'd fathered a son, a handsome boy who would now be approaching his thirtieth year. The hill women had begged for him to be groomed as their next king and, flattered, Jonathon had agreed. It had been a matter of grief to him that, from that time, he had never again got a son by any of his women.

The arched doorway opened and Wolfe smiled as he saw Esther waiting for him. She was one of Jonathon Summers' daughters but was small of stature and daintily formed. Her eyes glowed at him over the face veil and Wolfe knew she had watched his approach with eagerness.

Summers had discreetly turned a blind eye as the affair between Esther and Wolfe had blossomed. He was too much a man of the world himself to expect chastity from his offspring. But Esther was his favourite daughter and, though he allowed her great freedom, he made it quite plain that she was expected to remain with him always.

Wolfe became aware that Esther was staring past him, her eyes suddenly cold, to where Garnet was dismounting from the donkey. He held out his hand to help her but Garnet ignored the gesture. Damn her! She always made him feel boorish and ungallant.

Esther was slipping her small hand through his arm, her eyes wide as they looked up at him.

'Papa Summers has not been well,' she said softly. 'I believe his new wife saps much of his energy.' She smiled mischievously, her dark lashes covering her expressive eyes. 'He sleeps in the heat of the afternoon and I would prefer not to awaken him. Shall I bring you a cool drink, Wolfe?'

He shook his head. 'Not yet. Perhaps you would prepare a room for a guest.' He smiled as she pouted up at him, her lips rosy beneath the gauze that hung from a jewelled band bound into her hair. She was deliberately provocative, anticipating his eagerness to take her with him to his room. He recognized with a small shock of surprise that the urgency was no longer present.

Obedient as always, Esther glided away on sandalled feet, her long hair flowing behind her. And yet Wolfe had a definite impression that she was reluctant to leave him alone with Garnet.

He saw that she was still in the doorway, staring round her with large eyes, her soft mouth trembling. He was impatient with Garnet, sensing her disappointment in the Summers' residence. What had she expected, a mansion on the edge of the desert?

'Come inside for heaven's sake,' he said in a clipped voice. 'I know this isn't exactly what you are used to but at least it's better than the slave market.'

'I was thinking how charming it is,' her tone was chiding. 'As you say, it's not what I'm used to but that doesn't mean I can't enjoy the character of the house.'

He had misunderstood her again; she was constantly placing him in the wrong and it irked him.

'Wait here.' He gestured towards a chair. 'Esther will come for you presently.' He left her and strode along the corridor towards the back of the house where the sleeping quarters were situated. He felt thoroughly disturbed by the effect Garnet was having upon him. It was high time, he decided, that he put an end to the uncomfortable relationship.

Through Summers' open bedroom door, Wolfe caught a glimpse of his partner stretched out on his bed, eyes closed in sleep. Beside him lay a long-limbed girl, her brown skin gleaming with moisture. She waved a large flat leaf in a fan-like gesture so that small eddies of air fluttered the hangings on the bed. She smiled languorously at Wolfe as he passed and he realized she must be the new woman in Summers' life.

Inside his room, he stripped off his dusty clothes. It

would be good to rest in a real bed for a change. He gave a wry smile. What was wrong with him that he had not invited Esther to share the softness of the silken sheets with him? He lay down and closed his eyes, recognizing the fact that he was quite content to occupy the bed alone.

Garnet sat impatiently on the edge of her chair. She had been waiting for almost half an hour for Esther to reappear and show her to her room. Her heart twisted with anger as she imagined the beautiful young girl with Wolfe; perhaps even now she was in his arms.

She rose to her feet, moving swiftly across the faded carpet, reaching the door just as it opened. Esther stared at her with dark, hostile eyes.

'Your room is ready,' she said. 'Please follow me.' She made no apology for her long absence and Garnet pressed her lips together to prevent the angry words from tumbling out.

The room was very small and sparsely furnished, almost bare. A deal table stood beneath the boarded window and the wooden floor was uncarpeted. Against one wall was a narrow bed, the mattress sagging, the coverings patched and faded. Garnet stared around her, unable to conceal her dismay. She knew that Esther had deliberately placed her in the poorer part of the building, perhaps as far away from Wolfe as possible.

Esther smiled but her eyes were cold. 'We will eat our evening meal at six.' She put her palms together and touched them to her forehead. 'Enjoy your rest and come to the table refreshed.' The words were polite but the tone was flat, without emotion.

When she was alone, Garnet sank down onto the bed and the springs groaned in protest. She was coldly angry because, though it was apparent that the Summers' household was by no means luxurious, she knew that there was a homely comfort in the rest of the rooms that was entirely lacking in the one Esther had given her.

She looked around and saw there was not even a bowl of water provided for her to wash away the dust of her journey. With a sigh, she lay back against the uneven pillows, trying to find a little comfort, and, wearily, she closed her eyes.

The air was cooler when Garnet woke. She glanced out of the window and saw that the sky was losing its bright clear blueness. She sat up awkwardly and found that she ached all over. Her ride on the donkey had jarred every bone in her body and the discomfort of her bed was not conducive to easy sleep.

She left her room and found herself in a cool, dark kitchen. It was quite apparent that this part of the building was no longer in use because the wooden table was covered in dust and the stove had not been lit for many months. Garnet guessed that a new kitchen had been built and her suspicions about being placed in the poorest part of the house were confirmed.

She retraced her steps and heard the sound of voices coming from the large room at the front of the building. Here the carpets were new, the jewel colours gleaming in the light from the chandeliers that glowed and shimmered in the cool of the evening air.

She saw that dinner had already begun and Wolfe was seated at the long polished table beside Esther and he was leaning forward, intend on the conversation.

As she hesitated in the doorway, she saw the man who must be her host. He looked up and caught her eyes and a smile touched the corners of his mouth.

'Good heavens, an English girl and a beautiful one at that.' He rose and came towards her, his hair shining silver around. his bronzed, weather-beaten face. 'I'm Jonathon Summers and I extend to you the hospitality of my home for as long as you care to stay.'

He drew her forward. 'I think you might have told me, Wolfe, to prepare myself for such a dazzling beauty.' He held out a chair.

'Please sit down, my dear.'

Garnet glanced at Wolfe but he turned away from her, his head bent close to Esther's. She might as well be invisible for all the notice he took of her, Garnet thought with a rush of emotion. She became aware that Jonathon was speaking to her.

'Your father is one of King George's ministers, I understand,' he said conversationally. 'It is an honour to have you under my roof. I trust my daughter has made you comfortable?'

'Very.' Garnet wondered what he would say if she told him the truth. 'You have a lovely, elegant house, Mr. Summers.'

'Tut, tut, call me Jonathon, my dear, otherwise I shall feel very old.' He leaned back in his chair. 'Yes, the old place is beginning to look much improved these days,' he said. 'I have slowly but surely renovated the main rooms but there still remains a great deal to be done.'

'Wolfe has told me only the sketchiest of details about you. I hear you met under somewhat romantic circumstances.' Jonathon spoke lightly, breaking the strained silence.

'There is no romance between us,' Garnet said quickly. 'Mr. Surbiton is merely escorting me across the country, that's all. I'm not sure yet if he intends to take me to my aunt in Spain or home to England. Whichever course proves the most convenient for him, I dare say.'

'But you two would be so well suited,' Jonathon continued unabashed. 'You have such good connections and are beautiful into the bargain, a real gem of a lady if I might say so.'

'There is nothing between us, nonetheless,' Garnet repeated, aware of Wolfe's amused glances. She wished Jonathon would leave the subject alone but he seemed determined to go on with it.

'But you were alone in the desert,' he said softly. 'Did you not feel the magic of the golden land bring you closer together?'

Garnet looked down at her plate of rice, she remembered only too well lying in Wolfe's arms. But that was over and done with, a lapse on her part that she swore would not be repeated. She looked straight at Wolfe.

'I was not aware of any magic,' she said shortly. Her

eyes did not waver as Wolfe turned to look at her. His mouth moved silently and she made out the word 'liar'. Hot colour flowed into her face as she longed to slap him.

'Perhaps you would like to see my new sunken bath,' Jonathon said, and Garnet realized that he was aware of the tension and was deliberately changing the subject.

'That would be very pleasant.' She rose from her chair and followed Jonathon along the corridor to the right of the main building where the ceilings were higher and the furnishings more elaborate.

'This is my latest acquisition.' Jonathon drew aside gossamer curtains and Garnet stepped into a fairy-tale room resplendent with silk hangings and rich cushions, plump and shining. At the centre of the room was a low, marble bath and the water rippled constantly, sending a heavy perfume from its depth that pervaded the air.

Jonathon clapped his hands and a tall, well-built woman entered the room by another door. She bowed elegantly and smiled at Jonathon Summers, her dark eyes adoring. He gave her orders rapidly and she nodded, withdrawing silently. Jonathon smiled at Garnet.

'I shall show you the rest of my small establishment and, in the meanwhile, Coffee shall prepare the baths for you,' he smiled. 'That's not her real name but I cannot pronounce the one her parents gave her. She is beautiful, is she not?'

Garnet realized that Jonathon had more than a

casual interest in Coffee. She nodded her head. 'She's very lovely.'

He led her outside into the brilliance of the star-studded night. Along the edge of the fenced enclosure stood tall wooden sheds and to these Jonathon pointed.

'The store rooms,' he said. 'There I keep my rum and cigars, though I must confess that I trade in almost anything. Wolfe does not always approve but we make ourselves a comfortable living so why complain?' He spread his hands wide, smiling so charmingly that Garnet felt herself warming to him.

'What exactly is Wolfe's part in all this?' Garnet found herself asking. Jonathon shook his head.

'He provided the ideas at the outset and he had all the contacts. If there is cargo to be transported, Wolfe sometimes charters a ship in which he makes the deliveries. For myself, I will never leave the safety of my home. I have lived here ever since I was a child, the local natives trust me and I them. There is only one place that even I dare not venture.'

'Oh?' Garnet was by now only partly listening. She was wondering how Wolfe was getting along with the half-native daughter of her host. 'Please tell me about it.' She forced herself to listen to Jonathon.

'There is a tribe of women living in a small village surrounded by hills,' he said. 'They are large and strong, something like the Amazon women of South America, very beautiful too, I believe.' He sighed. 'My first-born son, a handsome child, was chosen by the women to be their next king. He has reigned now some fifteen years, the only male allowed in the village. He fathers the children of the maidens chosen as mothers.'

Garnet was intrigued by Jonathon's story and he had succeeded in gaining her undivided attention.

'Were you not reluctant to give up your son?' she asked, and her host nodded thoughtfully.

'Yes but then I imagined there would be other sons.' He shrugged. 'Instead, I continue to produce daughters. Some of them are taken into the village as warriors because of their size and strength.' He smiled wryly.

'Most of my lady friends are from a tribe a little distance to the north. They are called "the tall ones" and when you see Coffee you understand the name.'

'I do realize that Coffee is of exceptional stature,' Garnet agreed. 'But would she not object if she gave birth to a girl and the child was taken away from her?'

'You do not understand our ways,' Jonathon said with a smile. 'These children are the chosen ones, it is a great honour. Come, we will return to the house, your bath will be ready by now.'

Coffee was standing patiently waiting, a soft cotton robe over her brown arm. She inclined her head and spoke softly to Jonathon in a language Garnet could not understand.

He smiled and bowed to Garnet. 'Enjoy your bath, my dear.' He disappeared through the gossamer curtains and she heard his footsteps retreating along the corridor.

Coffee helped Garnet to disrobe and urged her forward, down the steps of the marble bath. The scented water was comfortably warm and lapped Garnet's shoulders like a caress. She felt herself relax completely as the dark-skinned girl began to rub her hair with oil, washing away the dust with firm movements of her long fingers.

Eventually, Coffee gestured to Garnet with a beckoning movement of her large hands and bent to pick up a cotton towel, holding it out with a smile.

Garnet felt deeply refreshed and wondered what herbs had been added to the water. It was as if, by some form of magic, her aches and pains had been washed away along with the dust.

Coffee helped to dry her long hair, the colour changing from dark chestnut when damp to rich, shining red waves that hung silkily on Garnet's shoulders.

Garnet drew on the bright, soft cotton robe. It was a simple garment mainly in white but with patterns decorating the neck and hem in rich, raw colours. Coffee nodded her head as though in satisfaction.

She took Garnet's arm and led her from the room, out through the curtains and along a dimly lit corridor. Coffee opened the large arched door and stood back for Garnet to precede her.

They were in a square courtyard lit by many flares. Insects flew across the flames making points of flashing light in the darkness.

Garnet saw Wolfe seated beside Jonathon on a high bench piled with deep cushions. His eyes flickered over her and then looked away as though he had not seen her.

Jonathon lifted his arm in greeting and Garnet went towards him, grateful for his interest in her. She sat beside him while Coffee lowered herself gracefully into a cross-legged position on a coloured mat near Jonathon's knees. His hand gently touched the dark hair in a brief gesture before he gave his attention to Garnet.

'You look very lovely, my dear,' he said genially. He had dressed himself in an ancient but imposing suit of nankeen with a waistcoat of faded silk. His hair was brushed until it shone startlingly silver under the flaring lights.

'Thank you, Jonathon,' she said, forcing herself to speak lightly, though she was acutely aware of Wolfe's heavy-lidded eyes staring at her, his gaze on the split neckline of the robe she wore. She drew back almost as though he'd touched her.

'Excuse me, my dear, I must see if that daughter of mine is ready to dance for us,' he smiled. 'I'll leave you in the capable hands of my partner. You and Wolfe have scarcely had time to pass the time of day since you arrived. There must be a great deal for you to talk about.'

When Jonathon moved away, it was as though she were alone with Wolfe. Garnet forced herself to meet his eyes and they were cold.

For an instant she was tempted to speak angrily to him, to demand to know why he was distant to the point of rudeness. She drew herself up and controlled the impulse.

Jonathon was returning with Esther and she was

beautiful in a garment of flame-coloured muslin caught close to her slender throat with a collar of rubies set in gold. Her long hair was swathed around her head like a turban and her eyes appeared larger and more brilliant, decorated liberally with kahl.

Softly, sensuously, drums began to beat on the stillness of the night air. Esther sprang, with cat-like grace, into the centre of the courtyard, her gown flaring around her as though flames from a fire licked her slender body. She moved her arms in sharp gestures so that her bracelets were in tune with the drums.

Slowly, Esther allowed the robe to slip from her shoulders down to her breasts and then let it fall softly to the ground.

She was covered now only with tiny metallic discs that barely concealed her breasts and the darkness between her thighs. She moved in a frenzied rhythm, her body swaying and bending, her long hair falling loose, covering her face.

Garnet was aware of Wolfe leaning forward as though eager not to miss a moment of the amazing dance and she felt dull and colourless compared to the vitality of the girl swaying before her.

Jonathon was speaking quietly to Wolfe, and Garnet could not help but overhear him.

'You have been very close to my little Esther in the past,' he was saying. 'And have had my full approval, Wolfe, just so long as you do not try to take her away from me.' He shrugged expressively. 'When I lose my attraction for women, my daughter will still love me.'

Garnet rose to her feet, longing to run away, unwilling to hear any more.

Esther had finished her dance and had fallen gracefully to her knees, arms upstretched towards the night sky, head flung back.

Breathlessly, she rose and came towards the bench, her eyes on Wolfe, her smile for him alone.

Jonathon was suddenly very jovial. 'Go away with you.' He kissed his daughter. 'Try your best to make me a grandfather.' He laughed as Esther caught Wolfe's hands, drawing him to his feet.

Garnet was unable to move. She stood watching the little scene, her heart beating rapidly, her hands clenched into fists. She saw Wolfe put his arm around the girl's naked shoulders, his dark head bent against her light one, his fingers caressing the brown flesh. She knew with a sudden crystal clarity that this was just what Wolfe wanted. He could take Esther and enjoy her without making any commitment. Love, to him, was nothing more than a meaningless word.

CHAPTER FIVE

Garnet woke slowly to the heat of late morning. She opened her eyes to find Esther standing beside her bed, a tray of tea balanced on her slender hands.

Garnet sat up carefully and the springs of the old bed creaked beneath her. She stared suspiciously at Esther, who was smiling with apparent friendliness as she placed the tray on Garnet's knees.

'Good morning.' Her voice was light, fast, over-eager, as though she felt she might be rebuffed. Her skin gleamed with the sheen of health and her dark eyes were bright. Garnet pushed away the image of the girl lying in Wolfe's arms.

'You are angry with me?' Esther said, pouting a little. Garnet almost tipped the glass of tea in her astonishment. She looked down into the amber depths, studying the slice of lemon with what seemed like avid interest as she tried to frame a reply.

'Why should I be angry?' she said at last. She looked up then, staring directly into Esther's face before looking round pointedly at the lack of comfort in her room.

'Oh, I did not mean all this.' Esther waved her hand

in an airy gesture. 'That is soon remedied, is it not? Today, I will see to it that one of the better rooms is cleaned and prepared for you.'

Garnet sipped the tea and waited for Esther to continue; she must surely come to the point of her visit before much longer. She was right.

'About Wolfe.' Esther examined her nails. 'What has happened between you?'

Garnet paused for a long moment before answering. She stared at the girl's flushed face, trying to see behind her innocent expression.

'I don't understand you.' Garnet placed the tea on the floor. It had been liberally laced with rum, which was probably the way Jonathon liked his morning drink served, but it was too sickly for her taste.

'You do understand,' Esther insisted. 'You love him, don't you?' She did not wait for a reply. 'That much I can see for myself, it is in your eyes whenever you look at him. What I wish to know is, what are his feelings, does he return your love?'

Garnet pushed aside the sheets impatiently. 'I do not wish to contradict you but you are entirely mistaken,' she said in a clipped tone. 'I do not wish to discuss the matter further.'

Esther sank down onto the bed, her dark eyes full of tears, so that she suddenly appeared very young and vulnerable.

'Wolfe did not come to me last night,' she said in a whisper. 'It is the first time since we became lovers that he has spent a night beneath this roof separate from me. Did he come to your bed?'

'Of course not,' Garnet said. 'I've told you, Esther, Wolfe and I are almost strangers, there is nothing between us, believe me.'

Garnet was suddenly sorry for Esther. 'Look,' she said slowly. 'He was probably tired; we had a difficult journey through the desert.' She wondered why she was putting herself in the absurd position of apologizing for Wolfe.

Esther was staring at her as she dressed. 'It is all right for you, a white woman. Wolfe could marry you and give you his sons.' She spread her hands wide, palms upwards. 'I have mixed blood, I know he will never take me for wife. In any event, my father wishes me to be always at his side.'

'Are you unhappy then?' Garnet asked, and Esther smiled, shrugging her shoulders daintily.

'I have always been content. I have had my father's affection and Wolfe's, too. All I need is a boy child and then he will grow up to be a fine trader.' Her smile vanished. 'But if Wolfe will not lie with me, I never have a child.'

Garnet turned away, suddenly uncomfortable. She would never grow accustomed to the open way Esther spoke about her relationship with Wolfe. But the girl was of a different culture, she had been raised in an atmosphere free of constraints. She had witnessed at first hand her father's association with many women and could not be blamed for her easy acceptance of lovemaking.

'You do not approve of me or my father,' Esther said quietly, and Garnet's colour rose as she realized her expression had betrayed her thoughts.

'I'm sorry,' she said in a low voice. 'It is nothing to do with me.' She shrugged. 'I am not used to your ways, yet, that's all.'

Esther rose from the bed and went to the door. 'Then you would not allow Wolfe to come to your bed?' Her tone was incredulous and Garnet bit her lip.

'It is customary in my country to wait until a man and woman are married,' she said, 'before they sleep together.' She knew she was avoiding the question but she could never explain to Esther or even to herself why she had allowed Wolfe to make love to her. But she had learned her lesson; she had found that he was a man without integrity. He took a woman as he took a glass of wine, but he would not amuse himself with her, ever again.

Esther was suddenly light-hearted once more. She caught Garnet's arm. 'So, Wolfe will never lay a finger on you unless he marries you.' She laughed merrily as though the idea was preposterous. 'I am very happy. Come, I will take you on a tour of my father's property, we will have great fun, you'll see.'

Garnet sighed. She might just as well go with Esther as sit alone in her room which by now was becoming increasingly hot and stuffy.

Esther walked on dainty feet along a network of corridors, her soft muslin gown fluttering around her ankles. Garnet followed her and found herself nearing a large, sunlit kitchen which was obviously newly built.

Copper pans lined the walls, hanging from large hooks, gleaming with cleanliness. The long table beneath a wide window was well scrubbed and the entire room smelled pleasantly of herbs.

'This is Fatima,' Esther said, and a large woman smiled up at Garnet from her seat near the fireplace. She was so big that her thighs overhung the stool which creaked as she moved.

Esther spoke to the woman softly, cajolingly, and a smile wreathed the plump, shining face. Fatima plunged her hand into the pocket of her spotless apron and brought out a large bunch of keys. She removed one and gave it to Esther who held it aloft, laughing in delight.

'Come, we go to my father's room,' she said softly. 'I shall let you see some of his treasures.' She turned as Garnet hesitated. 'He will not mind that we look, all will be mine one day, he tell me so often.'

Jonathon's room was near the front of the house. It was large with a high ceiling from which hung a chandelier of copper and wood. The bed was enormous with long trailing drapes surrounding it. Under the sheets, Coffee still lay, her arms stretched above her head.

Esther spoke to her sharply and the tall woman climbed slowly out of the bed, unabashed by her nakedness. She drew on a silk robe and moved away, leaving the door open as she glided out into the passage.

With a sharp exclamation of anger, Esther pushed the door shut.

'That woman, she thinks she owns my father.' She sighed. 'Coffee does not realize that she is only one of many.'

Esther pushed aside the curtains that surrounded the bed and drew out a tin box that was much used. The lid was dented in several places and the leather straps were worn and smooth.

'Look.' Esther threw back the lid and Garnet gasped as she saw a glittering array of gems intermingled with gold coins that struck sharp points of light across the room.

Garnet moved forward, intrigued in spite of the feeling that she was prying into something that was none of her concern. She touched a necklace of gold set with flashing garnets, lifting it from the cascade of jewellery, holding it against her throat.

'Charming,' Esther said, clapping her hands in delight. 'It looks just perfect against your white skin. Here let me fasten the clasp for you.'

She would listen to none of Garnet's protests, her fingers were quick and skilful, handling the delicate chain with ease. She stood back, eyes wide, admiring the affect.

'You are well named,' she said with a sigh of envy. 'The garnets pick up the colour of your hair as though the necklace was made for you. Please keep it.'

'I couldn't,' Garnet said quickly, trying to remove the heavy chain. 'Please open the fastening for me, Esther.'

'You must not worry,' Esther laughed, her white teeth gleaming against the golden brown of her skin.

'My father is very generous, he would wish you to take what you like.'

She walked quickly on dainty feet towards the door, turning to glance back at Garnet.

'Come, I shall show you my gowns. I shall have the pleasure of making you look even more beautiful. Please, do not disappoint me when I try only to be friends.'

Feeling as though she was being rushed along on a tide of events over which she had no control, Garnet followed Esther once more along the labyrinth of passageways.

'Come inside my room. Take what you will of my gowns. You see I have many more than I will ever need.'

Garnet sank into a low soft chair, noticing there was no lack of comfort in Esther's bedchamber. Fine carpet covered the floor, the pattern worn but still rich in colour. Plump cushions were placed against the walls that were hung with drapes of fine weave.

'Here, this is the gown for you.' Esther held a flame-coloured garment towards Garnet. 'Put it on, let me see how beautiful you are.'

Garnet sighed, 'I don't really see any point in all this, Esther.' She wondered where Wolfe was at this moment; she knew she must speak to him, force him to tell her when he intended to take her home. She didn't mind if he took her to Spain or returned her to England, just so long as she put as much distance between them as possible.

'Try the gown, please,' Esther begged. 'I only wish

to prove my friendship to you.'

Garnet's thoughts on that subject were uncharitably doubting but she could see no real harm in humouring the girl. Perhaps Esther really was making an attempt to make up for her initial hostility.

The gown was soft and silky, almost transparent as it fell over Garnet's slender body, whispering around her ankles in tiny folds.

'I must paint your eyes with kahl and perhaps a little antimony,' Esther said, her head on one side. 'Then, tonight, you will be a wonderful surprise to Wolfe and to my father.'

Garnet sighed, it seemed easier to allow Esther to have her own way than to protest. In any event, she felt not a little gratitude to Jonathon's daughter; without her, the hours would hang heavily indeed.

The heat of the sun was dying away as, later, Garnet made her appearance in the dining room. The two men were already seated and rose to their feet as she joined them at the table.

Esther fluttered into the room almost directly behind her in a simple white gown of watered silk with little in the way of embellishments. Beside her, Garnet suddenly felt ridiculously over-dressed.

Jonathon smiled at her kindly. 'You look stunningly beautiful, my dear.' He leaned a little closer. 'And I see you have accepted a small gift from my little store.'

Colour suffused Garnet's cheeks. 'Oh, I don't mean to keep the necklace,' she said quickly. 'It was just that Esther thought . . .'

'Not another word,' Jonathon interrupted. 'It is a

gift and if you refuse it I shall be heartily offended.'

Wolfe's eyes were coldly silver as he looked at her. Deliberately, he studied her appearance from head to foot and his arrogance set Garnet's teeth on edge.

'There is to be a little celebration later,' Jonathon's voice cut across Garnet's thoughts, and she turned to him with a smile.

He held a bowl of mutton pieces towards her. 'Take some, you will find the meat delicious. Yes, Coffee has arranged what the locals calls a *palavra* in honour of my guests. I feel sure you will enjoy it, Garnet.'

'Of course,' she murmured, scooping pilau onto the plate in front of her.

'I have attended your *palavras* before,' Wolfe said, with an irony that was not lost on his host. Jonathon laughed, spearing a piece of succulent mutton on his knife.

'Then you know what a delight you have in store, dear boy. To Garnet, all this is very new and I mean to show her how fine African hospitality can be.'

'Sometimes I believe you forget you were born in England, Summers,' Wolfe said amiably. 'Pass me a cup of rum, Garnet, would you?'

Startled to hear Wolfe speak her name, Garnet instinctively obeyed him, reaching out to lift the earthenware jug and pouring a generous measure of the thick, dark liquid into a silver goblet.

She sank back in her chair, furious with herself as she saw the light of laughter in Wolfe's eyes. He had issued a command and, like some mindless, besotted creature, she had responded.

When the meal was finished, Jonathon led the way into a large chamber that contained no furniture at all. The floor gleamed with marble tiles and plump cushions were scattered about the walls. Jonathon sank down cross-legged and, after a moment's hesitation, Garnet joined him. She was very aware of Wolfe's nearness as he sat on her left hand, his bare arm uncomfortably close to hers.

The plaintive note of a pipe sent chills along Garnet's spine. To the sound was added the muffled beat of a drum and the tension in the air could almost be felt.

From behind a curtain appeared the tall graceful figure of Coffee. She was swathed from head to foot in folds of cotton that wound from her neck up to cover her dark hair.

She was joined almost immediately by a man, taller even than she was. His face was darkly handsome, his movements lithe and supple.

The dancers circled for a moment, eyes meeting as though they were hostile strangers. The man, with a liquid motion of his hand, swept the covering from Coffee's head and her hair tumbled down her shoulders. They drew close together, bending and turning, thigh to thigh in a dance that depicted love.

Garnet felt tense, the display was disturbing, erotic and yet with an innocence that was charming. She saw the man catch the end of the cotton wrap and Coffee was spinning around, naked now except for a tiny piece of muslin across her slender hips.

The man bent over her and she drew away as

though in fear. He was winding silver chains around her body, capturing her until at last she melted against him.

The drums beat faster and Coffee was lifted high above her partner's head, her body arched and graceful, her long limbs gleaming in the candle-light. And then the dancers were gone, retreating silently behind the curtains, and the floor was as empty as though they had never been there.

Scarcely had Garnet caught her breath than the curtains were moving again and this time it was Esther who stepped out under the brilliant light from the chandelier. The simple white dress had been replaced by a necklace of coloured beads and a brief loincloth of leather. The long flaxen hair was plaited into tiny ribbons and, as the drums began to sound, Esther's supple body swayed to the rhythm.

The dance was slow, sensuous, calling for great control, and Esther's breasts gleamed golden brown under the flickering candles in the great chandelier.

A tall basket was brought and placed before her and Esther sank to her knees, her legs apart, the long column of her neck flung back as though in ecstasy.

From the basket, appeared the large head of a venomous snake and Garnet gasped in horror. Wolfe stared down at her in amusement, his eyes half closed.

'Don't worry, you will be quite safe.' His voice was dry as though he thought her dull and prudish. She forced herself to look away from him, back to the centre of the floor where Esther now lay flat out against the tiles.

The snake was moving towards the girl, winding around her body with sinuous swiftness. The wicked head pointed downwards between the gleaming thighs and it was as though the creature was taking possession of the woman and Garnet turned away from the sight, shuddering uncontrollably.

'Here, drink this.' Wolfe handed her a small silver cup and she drank the sweet white liquid from it in one quick swallow. She met his eyes and he leaned towards her, his hand on her shoulder.

'That will make you feel more at home,' he said, and she stared into his silver-grey eyes, not understanding the meaning of his words.

'What if we invite Garnet to dance for us,' Wolfe said aloud, and Jonathon Summers smiled in appreciation. Garnet was about to refuse abruptly, but somehow her power of speech seemed to have left her.

She relaxed against the silk cushions, her eyes meeting Wolfe's defiantly. He stared down at her, his face sensuous in the flickering candle-light.

She was beginning to feel strangely unreal and yet she knew with an inner triumph that she was desirable, a temptress. She pushed back her heavy fall of hair.

'I shall dance for you,' she scarcely recognized her own voice. She was on her feet, moving forward to the centre of the room, drifting on a cloud of mist. Dimly, she realized that Wolfe must have given her a potion that had strange powers, but the thought vanished as she felt the beat of the drum, deep within her as though it was her own heart.

Her body swayed to the rhythm that should have been foreign to her, but she was possessed by the wail of the pipe. Her hands moved over her body, cupping her breasts as though offering herself to a lover. The flame-coloured garment clung to her like a second skin as she danced faster, her long hair flowing wild around her face.

Something within her was reaching out to Wolfe as he sat forward, watching her intently, his heavy-lidded eyes unreadable. She did not understand the longing growing in her to lie in his arms, to feel his heart beat as one with hers. But her dance was for him alone.

Her hair was a curtain of tangled silk when, at last, she fell, breathless at Wolfe's feet. She heard the sound of clapping and triumph rose within her heart.

Wolfe was helping her to rise, his grip strong, almost painful on her arm. He was speaking to Jonathon who laughed as Garnet was led away. She tried to think clearly, but in the darkness of the passage she could not gauge where she was going. Wolfe was dragging her along and she heard herself whimper, but he took no notice. Indeed, his grip on her wrist tightened.

Then they were in his bedchamber. He kicked the door shut and drew Garnet towards the bed. He lifted her off her feet with ease and set her down on the silk sheets, kneeling beside her, his hand on the neck of the flame-coloured gown.

'Stop,' she said, but her voice was indistinct. Wolfe drew the gown away from her and his hands were on her naked breasts. She tried to push him away.

'Leave me alone!' She forced the words from her lips and she stared up into his face, shrinking from the anger she read there.

'I shall do just as I like with you,' he said grimly. 'Have you forgotten that you are my property, bought and paid for with my own money? I own you, do you understand?'

It was as though the primitive forces of the land of Africa were manifesting themselves within Wolfe's strong body. He pushed her against the pillows, his fingers at her throat.

'You are my woman,' he said. 'Whether you like it or not, you will share my bed.'

He was forcing her thighs apart and there was no tenderness in his touch. He was a monster, hungry for gratification. He thrust against her and her body yielded, betraying her. Wolfe smiled.

'You see, Garnet? You are not as indifferent as you pretend to be.'

She arched her back as his thrusting became stronger. His hands were bands of steel on her hips, drawing her closer, as though he would tear her apart in his passion.

She hated him. The thought spun round in her bewildered mind, a constant thread rising above the turmoil of her body which responded of its own volition. He was degrading her, using her as Jonathon Summers used Coffee. An amusement, nothing more.

She longed to strike out at him, but instead her arms were around his neck, enjoying the sensation of his smooth skin beneath her fingers. At the height of his passion, he cried out and she responded by clinging to him, holding him close, pressing his head between her breasts.

He was soon asleep. Garnet's mind was clearing and she sat up, staring around her in bewilderment. Tears ran along her cheeks into her mouth, tasting salt against her lips. He was no better than an animal. She hated him. He cared nothing for her feelings and, if she allowed him to go on using her, she would be crushed by him.

She rose from the bed and unsteadily wrapped herself in one of the silk sheets. She would return to her own small bare room, she would not remain in the same bed as Wolfe a moment longer than was necessary.

But once outside in the corridor, she realized she had little idea which direction she should take. She saw a light from an open door and moved gratefully towards it.

'My dear Garnet, what on earth are you doing wandering around like that?' Jonathon Summers was alone in his room. He rose from his bed, drawing on a robe of red silk.

'I seem to be lost.' She sat on his bed, staring up at him as though expecting him to put everything right. He sat down beside her and placed an arm around her shoulder.

'My dear,' he began softly. 'You are unhappy, there, cry on my shoulder, pretend I am your father.'

Garnet forced herself to control her tears. 'I'm sorry to be so foolish,' she said, unable to explain to him her grief at Wolfe's arrogant assertion that she was his property, to use as he chose. These were words she would never willingly repeat to the kindly old man at her side.

A sudden eerie wail of a horn shattered the stillness and Jonathon stiffened. He rose to his feet quickly, throwing off his robe.

'I must dress,' he said abruptly. 'We are being raided by the English sailors. Damnation, why was I not warned of this?'

The door opened and Wolfe stood there staring at Garnet as she sat on the bed with Jonathon behind her just beginning to draw on his breeches.

'Come. We must get out of here,' Wolfe said sharply. Jonathon spun round, colour suffusing his face.

'Wolfe my dear boy, this isn't what it appears,' he began, but he was cut short.

'There is no time for explanations and don't worry, Summers, I'm not laying any blame at your door.' He flung a robe at Garnet's feet. 'Get dressed, unless you want to be taken prisoner by the sailors.'

'Get away from here, both of you,' Summers said in a strained voice. 'If there is no time to conceal the evidence of the still, then I should not wish you, Wolfe, to be held. You would be much more valuable to me as a free man.'

Wolfe paused. 'It's more than just the still, this time, isn't it, Summers?'

'I've indulged in a small amount of slave trafficking, that's all. I'm not asking you to have any dealings with it, Wolfe, it is entirely my own concern.'

'Not now,' Wolfe said shortly. 'I am involved too.'
He moved to the door and Garnet hurried after him,
tying the cord of the heavy cotton robe around her
waist.

She was chilled as she heard a high scream coming
from the front of the house. She thought the voice was
Coffee's and for a moment she hesitated, unsure what
she should do. Wolfe caught her arm roughly and
drew her along the passage to the rear of the building.

'We should stop and help,' Garnet protested, but
Wolfe did not even pause in his stride.

'Would it help if we were detained by the sailors?' he
said, harshly. 'Our presence would only add fuel to
their suspicions.'

Esther was standing in the yard, holding the small
door in the corner of the wall open wide.

'Hurry!' she urged. 'You must not be found beneath
our roof.'

Beyond the gate was a large stretch of open, dusty
plain with only a few thin shrubs for cover. Wolfe held
Garnet's hand, running with her through the star-
spun darkness, and behind them Garnet heard a vol-
ley of shots. Her heart was pounding, she felt sure they
would be seen and fired upon mercilessly. Her
breathing was ragged and her legs trembled with
fatigue and terror by the time Wolfe drew her into the
sheltering safety of a rocky outcrop at the foot of the
hills.

Wolfe led the way into the darkness of a cave and
crouched on the ground. Garnet sank down beside

him, her head in her hands as she struggled to breathe.

'What will happen to Jonathon?' she asked at last, her heart still pounding uncomfortably fast.

'Nothing, if he moves quickly enough and if Esther keeps her wits about her,' Wolf replied. 'Why do you ask? Are you concerned about your latest conquest?'

'I don't know what you mean,' Garnet said, but in the darkness her face was hot.

'I mean it was strange I should find you both in bed together. Was it the necklace that persuaded you, Garnet? It must have been, why else would you lie with a man old enough to be your father?'

'You are vile!' Garnet was so angry she could hardly think straight. 'You must believe that not everyone has your own lack of moral strength. Jonathon was comforting me, that was all.'

She drew a deep breath. 'I don't know why I'm even bothering to explain to you.' She lay down on the soft, sandy ground, her hands beneath her head. She was cold now that the immediate danger was over. She began to shiver in her thin robe and she felt Wolfe move to take her in his arms.

'No!' she said fiercely. 'I'd rather die with cold than be obliged to you for anything.'

He did not answer her. She heard him roll over on his side, wrapping his coat around him, his breathing regular and even. She closed her eyes tightly, telling herself that never, in all her life, had she hated anyone so much as she did Wolfe Surbiton.

CHAPTER SIX

Wolfe was not asleep. He lay on the dusty floor of the cave, his back to Garnet but very conscious of her nearness. He heard her stir and knew she must be feeling the cold biting through her cotton robe. He half turned to take her in his arms but the thought of her running to Jonathon so shortly after she had been with him gave him a sick feeling in the pit of his stomach.

She was just the same as Lucia, he decided, for all her wide-eyed innocence. Show a woman a pretty bauble and she would do anything for a man. At least Lucia had been honest, she had not wrapped up her passion for him in fine sentiments. She desired him and had not been afraid to reveal her sensuality.

Wolfe realized he had been inconsiderate, even brutal, when he had forced himself upon Garnet. But she had taunted him, offering herself to him, exotic and beautiful as she had danced before him. She was entirely without inhibitions, and though he was perfectly aware that the potion he's administered was partly responsible, it could not bring out anything that wasn't there in the first place.

He lay on his back, staring up at the dimness of the cave roof. Garnet had the power to bring out the worst in him, her quiet dignity angered him. And yet she was like a fever in his blood, he wanted her and at the same time despised himself for his weakness.

He remembered the first time they had made love in the weed-covered lodge of the Bagger tribesmen. She had surrendered her maidenhead to him so sweetly, no doubt imagining herself with a gold ring on her finger and he with a ring through his nose. But he was not so easily caught. To him she was simply another woman, beautiful enough, but treacherous as they all were.

He gave up all attempts to sleep and rose to his feet, standing at the mouth of the cave staring into the distance. The sun was beginning to rise, colouring the dusty landscape with light and shade.

A movement caught his eyes, a gleam of steel from behind one of the dry shrubs. He became tense, as from all directions crouched figures emerged, approaching the cave where he stood. He thought for a moment that the sailors had tracked him from Summers' home, but these were women. They moved faster now and he saw they were tall and statuesque, their bodies garishly painted with chalk. Many of them were flaxen-haired and with a small shock he realized that these must be the daughters given by Summers to the tribe of warrior women who inhabited the hills.

They saw he was not armed and one, who appeared to be the leader, caught his arm, a wicked looking jambiel pointed towards his heart, the blade gleaming brightly in the sun.

'Out into the open.' She spoke English and her eyes, on a level with his own, were blue. She, like the others, was over six-feet tall, huge of breast and thigh, wearing only a haggu of twisted leather around her hips.

She gestured to one of the women who entered the cave, crouching like an animal, ready for the attack. Wolfe heard Garnet utter a small cry as she was woken from her sleep. He moved forward but the edge of the blade touched his throat warningly.

Garnet was blinking a little in the light of the sun, staring around her incredulously as though unable to believe her own eyes. Wolfe saw the leader of the woman lower her blade as it became apparent that the strangers represented no threat.

Although Wolfe was familiar with some of the native dialects, he could understand nothing of what the women were saying. He was grasped suddenly, his hands twisted before him, tied with leather thongs and, as he struggled furiously to free himself, the leader stepped forward. She raised her jambiel and the last thing he saw was the flat of the blade sweeping towards him. It crashed against his temple and he fell, unconscious, to the ground.

The climb up the winding stony path from the desert plane into the heart of the mountains was arduous and Garnet stumbled frequently, blinded by the sun that rose higher in the sky with every passing moment. The strange women had shown her nothing but kindness, lifting her when she fell, talking softly to her, unable to realize she could not understand them.

But Wolfe was still unconscious, being carried like a wild beast, hanging from a pole, secured by his hands and feet. She glanced round to see his head still hanging back, blood running from the wound in his temple, his dark hair trailing in the dust. She feared for his life.

It had not taken her long to realize who the women were. She remembered only too vividly Jonathon Summers telling her about the Amazon-like tribe of warriors to whom he had given his one son and many of his daughters.

The leader of the tribe bore a striking resemblance to Jonathon and, in contrast to the other women, her attitude to Garnet was one of hostility. She had spoken in English after she'd struck Wolfe to the ground, calling him a British dog, and yet her gaze had lingered upon him as he lay senseless on the ground.

Since then, she had remained silent, leading the warriors forward with decisive steps, as agile as a mountain goat. She seemed to know exactly where she was going, but to Garnet, it appeared as though they were heading towards a sheer wall of rock, that bounced the sun's heat back to the women as they toiled upwards.

Then a fissure, jagged, resembling a fork of lightning, opened up before them. The warriors passed through and the concealed door was closed behind them. Looking back, Garnet could scarcely believe there was an entrance in the rock at all.

She found herself descending a narrow pathway

and then, spread out before her, was an encampment, the like of which Garnet had never seen before. Green, verdant grass grew in the clearing that was surrounded by towering hills. Tall cypress trees, trunks twisted and gnarled, lined the perimeter. From one side of the hills, a spring ran crystal clear, tumbling downwards in a golden waterfall. At the foot of the hill was a long oasis and arranged around the water were rows of red leather tents.

Garnet watched as Wolfe was untied and carried away, still unconscious. She made a move to follow but the tribe leader caught her arm.

'You come with me.' She strode forward and held back a flap of skins, nodding to Garnet to enter the tent. Inside it was cool and pleasant with bright mats on the floor. The furnishing was sparse but well made.

'You may sit.' The leader indicated a low chair of smooth wood, beautifully carved in strange designs, and Garnet obeyed, sinking down, grateful to ease her aching body.

'I am Zeyd.' The woman clenched her fist and crossed her arm over her breast in greeting. 'My father is Jonathon Summers and you were a guest in his house. That's why I bring you here to the mountains.'

Garnet looked up at her in surprise. 'But how did you know about us?'

Zeyd smiled. 'I take my warriors to hunt for fennec foxes in the lower lands and we hear the horn that means the sailors come. We watch and see where you hide.'

'And what of your father?' Garnet asked, and Zeyd

shrugged, squatting down on the mat, her long legs crossed.

'He go with sailors to ship but they not keep him prisoner, they never do.'

Garnet was silent for a moment. 'How long will it be before Wolfe and I can go back to Jonathon's home?' A strange sense of uneasiness was building up within her. She longed to ask why Wolfe had been struck down but she did not dare.

'You do not leave,' Zeyd said. 'Once in the hills, you must remain, otherwise our encampment will no longer be a secret from the outside world.'

Garnet was on her feet. 'But you can't keep us here.' In her consternation, her fears were forgotten. 'Wolfe has a partnership with your father and you will not hold him against his will.'

Zeyd shook her head. 'I have not yet decided if he will live,' she said. 'Only one man is allowed to us women and he is my brother the King.'

She stared at Garnet's stricken face, allowing the full import of her words to sink in. She uncurled from the mat and stood to her height, an imposing figure, her large hand resting on the jambiel that hung at her side.

'You may serve a purpose,' she said. 'My brother might like to make you one of his wives so that you will bear white girls for the tribe.' She moved around Garnet, appraisingly. 'But it is possible he will think you too small in stature to be of any use.'

'But Wolfe,' Garnet said quickly. 'You can't really mean to kill hin?'

'I said I have not yet decided,' Zeyd spoke crisply. 'He is injured and may not survive his wounds. If he does, I shall consider what is to be done with him. He is a fine white man, of good stature and handsome features.' She frowned thoughtfully. 'I may find a reason for keeping him alive, we shall see.'

She went towards the entrance of the tent and left Garnet alone without speaking another word. A silence seemed to encompass the valley; only the drone of insects on the hot air disturbed the stillness.

Garnet pushed back the goat-skin flap of the doorway and the sun glared downwards, shimmering against the lake blinding her for a moment. She looked around desperately, not knowing where Wolfe had been taken or even if he was still alive. There was nothing she could do but wait. She sank down on the red and black mat and closed her eyes but, weary though she was, she could not rest.

She tossed and turned for what seemed hours, her eyes dry and burning, her limbs aching. At last, she heard the whisper of footsteps in the grass outside and a woman entered the tent, staring down at Garnet with wide, dark eyes.

'Myrena,' she said, and placed her clenched fist across her full breasts. She was heavy with child and it was with much difficulty that she settled herself on the mat beside Garnet. She took a copper bracelet from her arm and, with a smile, handed it to her, nodding encouragement as Garnet slipped it over her wrist.

'Myrena,' she said again, pointing towards herself. It was clear she wished to be friendly and Garnet returned her greeting, placing her fist across her bodice and murmuring her own name.

'Garnet,' she said softly. 'I am Garnet.' The two women stared at each other and Myrena put her head on one side in an attitude of thoughtfulness. She touched the robe Garnet wore and tugged at it, apparently wishing Garnet to remove it.

After a moment's hesitation, Garnet rose to her feet and untied the robe, allowing it to fall at her feet. Myrena scrutinized her impersonally before nodding her head. Without moving from her chair, she called out in a loud harsh voice and the words were foreign and ugly to Garnet's ears. Immediately, several women entered the tent and stood waiting for instructions.

Myrena smiled reassuringly at Garnet as the women led her outside, into the glare of the late sun. Garnet knew that the tall guards moving along beside her meant her no harm; they continually smiled, touching Garnet's hair, exclaiming to each other in their strange, harsh tongue.

She was led towards the waterfall and, as she entered the cool tumbling stream, her skin and hair were rubbed with a soft, oil substance that washed the dust away at once, leaving a scent of herbs that was clean and pleasant.

One of the women laughed delightedly, placing her own brown, muscular arm next to Garnet's slender, white shoulder, chattering excitedly. They were like great children, Garnet decided, gentle and kind in spite of their war-like appearance.

At last, Garnet was taken back to the tent and dressed in a haggu of twisted leather. Around her neck was hung a string of bright beads and tinkling bracelets were placed on both her arms. It seemed that she was being accepted as one of the tribe.

There was an air of festivity about the camp, a great fire burned at one end of the clearing and huge portions of meat crackled and steamed on a crude spit. An awning of gold and scarlet cloth was being erected in the centre of the verdant ground between the tents, and Garnet saw that it was decorated with gleaming gems that were arranged in a pattern representing the rays of the sun.

Garnet was left alone, free to wander at will. She strolled through the tents, deliberately looking around, trying to find where Wolfe had been taken. She came to a long, rectangular tent and saw women working, babies strapped to their backs. They toiled over goat skins, tanning and dying the leather with dark red clay.

This appeared to be the camp nursery. Toddlers wandered between the kneeling women, some of them with the striking contrast of flaxen hair against dark skin. Occasionally, a woman would stop whatever she was doing and sit cross-legged on the ground, feeding her baby.

Garnet retraced her footsteps, despairing of ever finding Wolfe. She bit her lip, wondering how serious his wounds were. He had looked so pale and weak from loss of blood as he had been carried into the valley.

The harsh strident sound of a gong being struck repeatedly reverberated along the rows of hills surrounding the camp. Garnet stared around her, suddenly apprehensive. Women were leaving their tents, making for the centre of the clearing, and there seemed little choice open to Garnet except to follow them.

Work on the awning had been completed and two intricately decorated chairs stood beneath its shade. With a small shock, she saw that the bases of the chairs were polished human skulls that seemed to grin hideously.

Myrena, garbed now in a flowing cloak of black and red cloth, took her place beneath the awning, sitting on the highest of the two chairs. She clapped her hands and, slowly, drums began to beat in a steady tattoo.

Into the clearing came a large man, flanked by two of the women warriors. His hair gleamed in the sunlight and Garnet knew that this was the son Jonathon Summers had spoken of. The likeness was indisputable. He took his place alongside Myrena and the couple exchanged greeting, fists clenched, arms across breasts.

The drum beats grew faster, louder, and a hush of expectancy hung over the crowd of waiting women. Turning, Garnet saw a procession of young girls, most of them no more than fourteen years of age. At the front, dressed in flowing white robes, stepped an older girl with jet black hair. She walked with measured tread as though she was in a trance. Her eyes apparently saw nothing and her head was unnaturally erect. Garnet guessed that she was not one of the descendants of Jonathon Summers; she had no resemblance whatsoever to him or his son.

When the girls were beneath the awning, Myrena and the king rose to their feet. A great sound of chanting filled the air as the man's robes fell from his magnificent body.

Myrena was kneeling at his feet, removing the haggu of red leather from his strong loins. He was a giant of a man, as he stood arms raised, eyes closed, chanting along with the rest of the tribe.

Myrena had turned her attentions to the dark-haired girl and was untying the cords of the white robe. Beneath it, the girl was completely naked and her brown skin shone as though oiled. Her face was quite expressionless and it was clear she was under the influence of some potion that left her apparently awake, while dulling her senses.

The procession was moving now, the king alongside the naked girl. Behind them, the young maidens of the tribe followed at a discreet distance. They walked in the direction of the waterfall and, as Garnet watched, the young girl was led beneath the golden flow of water, and laid flat upon the rocks.

The king leaned over her and it suddenly became clear to Garnet what the ceremony was. The king was to have a new bride and the nuptials were to take place before the entire tribe.

The golden water flowed over the king's naked body, cascading down his broad shoulders and along the flat planes of his stomach. The two bodies were moulded together as though cast in liquid bronze.

When it was over, the king moved from beneath the waterfall and Myrena waved him away as though he were no longer of any importance. The bride was drawn to her feet and a robe wrapped around her naked shoulders. She still stared blankly ahead, her face expressionless as she was led from the scene of the festivities.

The drums were beating in a frenzy of rhythm, then the women began to dance, the warriors waving glinting jambiels towards the gleaming sky above them.

'You like our fertility dance?' Zeyd had appeared beside Garnet on silent feet, her eyes alight with spiteful amusement. She stared down, her eyes appraising, and Garnet moved uneasily.

'I think my brother the king shall take you as his next bride,' she said coldly. 'He is father to so many of our young girls that it becomes difficult to find him fresh maidens.'

'I am entirely unsuitable,' Garnet said quickly. 'You said yourself I am too small of stature. In any event, I do not wish to be your brother's bride.'

'What you wish is not of importance,' Zeyd said indifferently. 'And though it is true you are inferior as a woman, I think you will amuse Kabel, my brother.'

'Please, allow Wolfe and I to leave your camp,' Garnet said quickly. 'We would return to the home of your father and say nothing about this place to anyone, I give you my word.'

Zeyd shook her head. 'No, that is impossible. The white man is very sick, perhaps unto death, and if he is spared by the gods of the sun, then I mean to make him the new king. Kabel's power wanes and fresh blood is needed for my people to survive.'

Garnet looked around her as though searching for a way of escape. Zeyd smiled, her eyes cruel, her mouth a thin line.

'The only ones to leave the valley, ever, are the warrior of the tribe. We go search for meat and we trade with other tribes but there is no escape for such as you. I need post no guards. You will never discover the secret of leaving here.'

She strode away, her long, golden legs covering the ground rapidly. Garnet knew Zeyd was right, the crack in the rocks would be too difficult for her to find alone and, in any event, she could not leave Wolfe behind.

She returned to her tent and sat down on the small coloured mat, her spirits low. There seemed no way out of the terrible situation she so unexpectedly found herself in.

'Oh, Wolfe, what is going to become of us both?' she whispered. Tears filled her eyes as she lay her head wearily upon her arms. From outside, the beat of the drums seemed to rise to a crescendo as though mocking her.

CHAPTER SEVEN

The festivities continued well into the night and it was only when the broad bands of early sunlight streaked the sky that the camp fell into a sleeping silence.

Garnet sat wide-eyed, staring before her. She could not rest for the fear that gnawed and chewed within her. If only she could see Wolfe, reassure herself that he was recovering from the blow dealt him by the warrior leader. She rose from the eskim, the brightly coloured sleeping mat held no comfort for her, and went slowly to the doorway of the tent. Outside, the morning air was pleasantly cool. A lone raven sent out a shrill throaty call and Garnet shivered as though she had come face to face with an evil omen.

From a distant tent came the thin wail of a baby, but no one stirred. She walked on tiptoe through the soft grass, her eyes darting from side to side, searching for something that would tell her where Wolfe lay.

On the very edge of the camp under the shadow of an overhanging rock, she saw a tent set apart from the rest. The skins were undyed, retaining the grey, marked with brown, of the skin of the mountain goat. The bars that crossed the four upright poles of the tent were patterned with cross hatchings burned into the wood.

Cautiously, she approached the entrance and her breath almost left her as she saw Wolfe, spread out on an eskim, his eyes closed, a large white cloth swathed round his head.

She crawled nearer to him and saw that he was very pale with deep violet shadows beneath his dark lashes. She put her cheek against his and he was cold. His breathing was shallow and his heartbeat faint. Garnet felt a sudden urge rising within her. She wanted to hold him close, cradle him in her arms and beg him to recover.

Behind her she heard a movement and an old woman with faded eyes stared at her suspiciously. She spoke in a harsh voice, and though Garnet could not understand her words, the meaning of them was very clear as she swept her thin arm towards the doorway.

Garnet, with a last anguished look in Wolfe's direction, fled back to her own tent and sank down onto the eskim, her hands clenched together as she fought against the tears welling in her eyes. She would see Zeyd and demand that Wolfe be given attention so that he might at least have a chance of recovery.

The camp was stirring into life. She heard a woman singing as she went about her duties and the aroma of cooking meat filled the air.

Myrena brought Garnet a breakfast of rice and raisins and she smiled as she seated herself carefully on the eskim, placing the bowl of food on the low table.

Garnet was hungry and, even as she dipped her fingers into the warm rice, she felt guilty because she could eat while Wolfe lay unconscious in his tent. Afterwards, she felt stronger however, and she realized it was vital that she keep up her strength.

Myrena shifted her position awkwardly, her hands supporting her swollen body. Her raw-boned face was drawn with weariness and it was apparent even to Garnet that the birth of the woman's child was imminent.

Myrena caught her glance and nodded, pointing to her body. She frowned, trying to communicate with Garnet. She held her arms as though cradling a child and rocked them slowly back and fore.

'Soon,' she said. 'Baby come soon.' She did not look happy and Garnet wondered what could be wrong. Myrena was the queen of the tribe, Kabel's chief wife. Surely a baby would improve her standing even further.

Myrena licked her fingertip and made a drawing on the surface of the table. The crude figure was that of a boy child and Myrena took the jambiel from her haggu and stabbed at the drawing. Garnet gasped with horror, realizing suddenly what Myrena was trying to tell her. A boy child would be destroyed at birth. This explained why all the occupants of the valley were female. Myrena touched the roundness of her body and pointed to the drawing.

'You fear you will bear a boy child, is that it?' Garnet said softly, and Myrena nodded, rocking herself to and fro, hands around her large knees, her eyes staring downwards.

Garnet put a hand tentatively on the queen's shoulder, in an effort to comfort her.

'Perhaps after all your baby will be a girl,' she said, and Myrena nodded her head, but it was clear from her expression that she was not convinced. After a moment, she struggled to rise and, once on her feet, gestured to Garnet, her large hand pointing towards the doorway. 'Come,' she said slowly.

The sun had risen in a cloudless, brilliant sky now and the shadows cast by the tents were long and black. Garnet followed Myrena's large form across the grass that surrounded the oasis and was surprised to find herself in a part of the camp she had never seen before.

Behind a jutting craggy rock was an enormous tent built on four large tree trunks and consisting of at least a hundred animal skins dyed red and beaded with stones that shimmered in the sunlight. Skulls decorated the doorway, polished and bleached white.

Inside, the floor was covered with deep rich carpet and against the far wall stood an elegant four-poster bed with wide cool hangings of muslin. Upon it, deeply sleeping, was stretched the king, his long golden limbs relaxed, his hair falling across his serene brow. He was handsome enough to stir any woman, Garnet thought. She could see how the young girls of the valley would deem it the greatest of honour to be his chosen woman.

She gasped, suddenly realizing that she had been brought to the king for a purpose. She looked up at

Myrena who, sensing her feelings, placed a hand upon her shoulder.

The queen spoke in her harsh tongue to Kabel and he sat up, staring at Myrena with full awareness. It was as though he had been awake all along, so alert and clear were his eyes.

Myrena bowed awkwardly and withdrew and Garnet's mouth was dry with fear. She almost turned to run but his voice stopped her.

'Wait,' he spoke English clearly, without the halting uncertainty that marked his wife's speech. 'I will not hurt you.'

He rose slowly, beckoning her forward, and she hastily averted her eyes from his nakedness.

'You stayed at the house of my father, Jonathon Summers,' Kabel said. 'Tell me of him, he must be a fine man.'

'He is,' Garnet said, a slender hope warming her heart. 'Perhaps we could go to him. I know he very much regrets losing you, his only son.'

Kabel shook his head. 'No one can go back. Once in the valley, the only way out is death.' He stared at Garnet searchingly.

'The white man, he lays near to the cave of death so my sister Zeyd tells me. We wait for the sun god to take his spirit. This we do in honour of my father who was this man's friend.' He smiled. 'Otherwise Zeyd would have left him for the birds to pick clean.'

He reached out a large hand and caught Garnet's wrist. 'But come, let me look upon you. For you at least there will be happiness in the valley of women. You will become my bride with great ceremony, Myrena will paint you and the women will give you chine which is a potion that takes away pain and fear. I will make you mother of my daughters.'

He drew her down on the bed beside him, his hand covering her breast. 'You are so small,' he said in wonder. 'But I think you will be very sweet.'

Garnet stared at him, trying not to reveal her horror at his intimate handling of her body. Kabel was wrapped up in his own thoughts.

'I must have a healthy girl child. There is nothing I would not give you, if you bear me a daughter.'

He frowned. 'I have been failed many times of late, the maidens do not bear me children. It is they who are at fault, not Kabel.'

He tipped her backwards and Garnet gave a small cry as his hands pulled at the slender haggu, drawing it away from her. Kabel ran his hands over her hips and down into her thighs. He nodded as though satisfied and a smile curved his lips.

'You have good bones, you carry children well. I soon fill you up with my baby.'

He called out loudly, clapping his hands together, and Myrena returned, inclining her head deferentially to her king. She smiled at Garnet as the king spoke of his approval. It was apparent that the queen imagined she was helping her guest to achieve her heart's desire. To the women of the valley, there was doubtless great honour in being one of Kabel's chosen women.

The main meal of the day was eaten in the open as the sun was dying in the blazing sky. The women, with the exception of the warriors, spent several hours cooking and preparing the food, which was served in platters and bowls of carved wood.

Pride of place was given to Zeyd and her band of women hunters who sat cross-legged before the table which was little more than a bench of rough planks raised on shaped stones.

The women who had grown too old for either hunting or child-bearing waited upon the younger members of the tribe. These sisters wore long white robes tied with black cord. Hoods covered thinning hair affording protection from the heat.

Of the king, there was no sign. It seemed his rare appearances were confined to special ceremonies such as the one of bridemaking that Garnet had witnessed.

When at last the meal ended, Zeyd rose to her feet and lifted her arms. This was apparently the signal for the tribe to disperse, and with a great deal of chatter in their strange tongue, the women began to clear away the remains of the food.

From the perimeter of the camp, came the haunting sound of a pipe being played, the notes rising and falling on the still air. The soft rhythm of drums throbbed into life and it seemed that the time of leisure was beginning.

'You like our way of life?' Zeyd appeared at Garnet's side, hands on large shapely hips, hair flung back, hanging loose now on her shoulders.

'It's very peaceful here,' Garnet answered. 'I can see that it suits you valley people very well.'

'But not you?' Zeyd's eyes were shrewd as they

rested on Garnet. 'But you will grow accustomed to it, you have no choice.'

She lifted her arm and pointed. 'You see the sisters, the old women? They are the original tribeswomen. At one time they were great hunters, the greatest in all Africa. One of them was mother to Kabel. She lived with Jonathon Summers for many suns until he tired of her. When that happened, she returned to the valley and to the old way of life where women rule.'

'And now she waits at table with the other older women?' Garnet said, and her tone of irony was not lost on Zeyd.

'She waits upon no one.' Her voice was sharp. 'She is revered by all. She a woman of great learning, taken by the English missionaries when a baby. Now we ensure that sort of accident no longer happen, only warriors leave the valley.'

'Zeyd,' Garnet's voice was urgent. 'Tell me what is going to happen to Wolfe?'

The tribe leader glanced away quickly. 'I do not know, only the god of the sun knows if he will live or die.'

'But if he recovers, what do you intend to do with him?' Garnet felt breathless as she waited for Zeyd's answer. She saw a host of varying expressions fleeting across the face of the huntress. At last, Zeyd shrugged.

'I have not made up my mind,' she suddenly seemed angry. 'It is not for you to question the tribe leader. You will be silent on the subject, do you understand?'

She moved away on graceful legs, her steps light

and swift, her long hair blowing back from her broad shoulders. She disappeared into the forest of tents and Garnet bit her lip, wondering if she dare go to the place where Wolfe lay sick, dying.

At last, she decided to wait for darkness. The moon slid softly from behind the clouds, bathing the oasis in silver and casting strange patterns of light between the tents.

Wolfe was lying quite still. He was alone and Garnet crept nearer to him, lifting his head up in her arms. She held a little water to his lips and dabbed her damp fingers across his forehead. It seemed that he would respond to nothing. She pressed her lips against his, begging him silently to live.

It seemed her prayers were answered, the dark eyelashes flickered and then he was staring up at her in the shaft of moonlight from the entrance of the tent.

'Wolfe!' Garnet held the bowl of water nearer to his lips and he drank thirstily. He was too weak to speak, and after a moment, his eyes closed once more.

Garnet knew what she must do. She would not sit waiting as Zeyd did for the intervention of the sun god. It was apparent that Wolfe had been given no food or water since he had been brought unconscious into the valley. But now she would go to him each night, she would coax him back to life if it were humanly possible to do so.

She kissed him and then crept from the tent. She would return just before dawn and help him to drink more water that would restore the life-giving moisture to his body. A sense of determination filled her, as she made up her mind that once Wolfe was strong again then together they would find their way out of the valley of women.

Sleep came slowly and then it was unrestful, filled with dreams and fears. She saw again the dark feather of the raven and the bird seemed to call out a warning to her as she was led beneath the waterfall where a smiling Kabel waited for her. She awoke suddenly, bathed in perspiration, and she knew by the heat in her tent that the sun was already up.

Outside, there was a stillness that told her the women of the camp were not yet about their business. She might yet be in time to tend to Wolfe. She raced through the grass that touched her bare legs like cool fingers. Over her shoulder hung a girby that bulged with fresh, sparkling water.

Wolfe's eyes opened as she held the water to his lips. The old light was in the blue-grey depths once more and Garnet smiled down at him eagerly.

'You are going to be all right,' she spoke softly, reassuringly to him. 'I shall come to you each night and morning and, look I shall hide the girby of water here, beneath your coat.'

She knelt beside him, untying the cloth that was matted with blood from round his head. She winced as she saw the open wound, fearing to bathe the tender flesh lest she start the bleeding again.

Wolfe's fingers curled around hers and a fleeting smile crossed his face. On an impulse, Garnet bent and kissed him. Then she was on her feet, retreating from the tent.

Her feet were swift as she crossed the verdant grass-land and her heart sang with joy. She would care for Wolfe and nurse him back to health. Once he was well and strong again, he would find a way out of the sweet valley that had become their prison.

CHAPTER EIGHT

Garnet was resting in the heat of the afternoon as was the custom in the camp. She lay on her eskim, eyes closed, trying desperately to ease the tension in her limbs. But however hard she tried, sleep would not come. She could not get the image of Wolfe's pale drawn face out of her mind.

For two days now, she had watched him making a slow recovery. This morning before the sun was up, he had even managed to eat a small portion of rice and raisins. She had at last found the courage to bathe and cleanse his wounds but he had lost a great deal of blood and was still very weak.

From the clearing outside came a loud, blood-curdling scream. Garnet sat up, her heart beating swiftly with fear. She rose and peered through the flap of the tent. The women of the tribe were gathering together and a scuffle seemed to be taking place very near to where Garnet crouched.

Two gargantuan guards were holding a woman, tying her hands behind her back with leather thongs, forcing her to kneel upon the ground. She hung her head now, the spirit gone from her, and she no longer struggled to escape.

Zeyd towered over her, questioning her in harsh tones, but the girl refused to answer. A cup was brought and the prisoner forced to drink, and even though she tossed her head from side to side in terror, the liquid was poured into her mouth.

Garnet moved out into the open, her pity for the girl lending her courage. She stood beside the tribe leader and forced a note of authority into her voice.

'What is the woman being punished for, what crime has she committed?'

Zeyd's eyes were like steel. 'This is tribal law. Hirfa is with child and she has not been made bride to the king.' She shook back her long hair and her hand fingered the jambiel at her side.

'There are no other men in the valley,' Garnet persisted. 'The child must be Kabel's.'

'No!' Zeyd's voice was harsh. 'Hirfa warrior, she trusted outside valley. She must have found lover from another tribe, we find out truth when she drink chine.'

The kneeling girl was still now, liquid trickling from between her pale lips. On a command from Zeyd, she was hauled to her feet where she stood passively, staring before her. Her eyes were dull as she answered the tribe leader's questions. At last, Zeyd seemed satisfied and Hirfa was dragged roughly away.

'What do you intend doing with her?' Garnet asked, and she knew the answer before Zeyd spoke.

'The punishment for such a crime is death,' she said with finality. 'Hirfa, as a warrior, was trusted and loved. Now she pay the price for betraying our laws and following her own passions.'

Drums began to throb with a low beat of urgency and Garnet saw the warriors assembling in the clearing. Zeyd glanced impatiently at the white woman.

'You stay, look after our queen, her time is near. When the baby is to be born, the elder sisters will attend Myrena. I go now, search for man who defile our tribe.'

As the women left the valley, climbing the winding path to the mouth of the mountain, Garnet shivered, pitying the man who was to be hunted. He had little chance of escaping from the wrath of Zeyd and her women warriors.

Later, as darkness fell over the camp, Garnet prepared a bundle of food, filling a girby with fresh water from her own earthenware jug. She would go to Wolfe, perhaps coax him to eat a little.

No one saw her step warily from her tent into the great dark shadows that covered the ground. The camp was empty of warriors and the rest of the women were too busy to keep a watch.

Wolfe was awake, his eyes were clear, and Garnet sighed with relief as she saw he was much improved.

'Here, let me help you to eat a little of the rice and fruit I saved for you.'

She held his head carefully on her knees, placing small quantities of food between his lips. He was still pale, with large shadows in the hollows of his cheeks, but he was growing stronger. She could already see a change in him from the half-dead man he had been when he had entered the valley.

His lips moved but there was no sound, and Garnet leaned closer to him, her heart wrenched with pity.

'Hush. Do not try to talk until you are stronger. We are safe enough here for the moment.'

Garnet heard the rustle of grass outside the tent and withdrew into the shadows, hiding herself behind the goat-skin flap that served as a door. One of the elderly sisters entered and approached the eskim where Wolfe lay.

She bent over him and his eyes were closed. The woman touched his forehead with the back of her hand and then moved away, satisfied that he was unconscious.

She retreated from the tent, muttering to herself, fingering the beads that hung from her waist as though invoking the spirits to guard her. After a moment, Garnet crept once more to Wolfe's side.

'I must go,' she whispered. But his eyes remained closed, the long dark lashes curling against his pale cheeks. She bent and kissed his mouth and then stumbled out into the night.

Myrena was waiting for her beside her tent, eyes straining in the darkness. She held out her hand as Garnet appeared and the look of relief in her face lit up her drawn features.

'It's time,' she said. She held Garnet's arm, drawing her towards the royal tent. 'Come, Kabel not here, only me.'

She leaned over the great bed, her face twisted with the pain that seared her body. Garnet gasped as she realized Myrena was experiencing the pangs of her labour, struggling with stoicism to give birth to her child.

She forced herself to remain calm. 'What must I do, Myrena?' she asked softly, her hand gentle on the queen's shoulder.

The pain subsided and, panting, Myrena rose from the bed, giving Garnet a length of cord and a blade. She gave a turn of her hands moving them in such a way that was clearly a demonstration of how the child should be brought into the world.

'I will do my best,' Garnet said, attempting to sound reassuring though her heart was beating swiftly with apprehension.

She brought a bowl of water and placed it near the bed just as Myrena gave a further cry of distress and crouched down on the covers, screwing her eyes tightly together in her strenuous attempt to give birth.

'Just a little harder,' Garnet gasped as she caught the infant's head, turning it gently, allowing the shoulders to emerge. With a rush, the child was born. Myrena lay back panting and Garnet looked down in wonder at the perfect being lying in her arms. Tiny fingers began to move slowly, like a butterfly opening its wings. The rosebud face crumpled and the baby began to cry.

Myrena lifted her head, recovering from her ordeal already. Garnet held up the infant and the queen's face puckered as though she would scream out in her despair. Her instincts had been right. She had given birth to a boy.

Myrena was a strong woman upon whom the effort of child-bearing left little impression. She fed the baby and then rose and dressed herself in a flowing black and red gown tied with a silver cord. She stared at Garnet for a long moment, her eyes pleading for help, and when she went outside into the darkness of the night, Garnet felt bound to follow.

Myrena was sure-footed as she made her way up into the rocky hills that surrounded the valley which itself rested on a plateau high in the mountains. Behind her, Garnet stumbled in the darkness, wondering at the strength that forced the queen onwards.

They halted at last and Myrena led the way into a cave, the entrance to which was hidden by a riot of bushes. At once, the mother began to fashion a bed for her child, working quickly and surely in the darkness. She made a nest of brush and dried grass, lying her baby carefully against the softness, kissing his sleeping forehead in a gesture of farewell.

She hurried out once more into the night and Garnet could hardly keep pace with Myrena as she descended once more into the heart of the valley.

She did not return to her tent at once but, gesturing to Garnet, led her to a small plot of freshly dug earth that was screened from the rest of the camp by a line of thick brush. Crouching, Myrena turned some of the soil with her large hands and finally placed a marker of rough stone over the small oblong of earth.

'Tomb,' she said. 'Resting place of dead souls.' She brushed the earth against her robes and Garnet realized what Myrena was going to do. She intended to tell everyone her child had died at birth.

Once inside her tent, Myrena sank down onto the bed, her face pale, small beads of moisture diamonding her dark brow.

'Bring me drink,' she said, her voice little more than a whisper.

Garnet's hands trembled as she held the cup to the queen's lips. She knew that Zeyd was safely out of the valley, but where was the king.

'Kabel?' She said to Myrena. 'Where is he?'

'He go to sacred circle when birth begin, he pray for girl but gods no longer hear him.' She looked at Garnet shrewdly.

'You fear him, you no wish to be his bride?' She said, her voice questioning.

'I cannot be his bride,' Garnet answered. She looked down at her hands. 'And yes, I am afraid of him.'

'All shall be well,' Myrena said. 'You will take my son. Carry him to Jonathon Summers. I shall show you the way.'

Garnet stared at the queen in consternation. This was just the sort of opportunity she had been waiting for but it had come at the wrong time. She could not leave without Wolfe.

'I will do as you ask,' she said at last. 'But not until the white man is recovered. I cannot leave him behind, but I shall ensure your son's safety. The white man will protect us both on the journey, you must see the sense of what I say.'

Myrena shook her head sadly. 'If gods spare him, he

will stay. Zeyd make him new king, Kabel fail too many times to make daughters.' She pointed to the empty crib beside the large bed. 'This make it worse for him,' she shrugged. 'A dead girl or live boy, both mean disaster for tribe.'

There was a sudden noise outside in the camp where the morning light was spreading pale fingers across the grass, turning it from grey to rich green.

Myrena waved her hand. 'Go, see what happens,' she said. 'I think Zeyd has returned.'

The clearing was filled with women, some of them roused from sleep, hair-tousled, eyes dull. One woman had a baby on her breast as she hurried from her tent, eyes wide with curiosity.

Between two women guards hung a man, a limp creature of small stature who was obviously terrified by the might of his captors. For him, Hirfa had risked everything and she had lost. The women jeered at the man's nakedness, gathering around him, pointing in ridicule.

Hirfa was led towards her lover. The effects of the chine had worn off and she stared with anguished eyes as the man was bound hand and foot.

The women warriors, breastplates gleaming, surrounded the girl and she too was forced to the ground, her arms twisted cruelly behind her back and tied with cords of leather.

'What news of the queen,' Zeyd stood beside Garnet, her eyes cold, her voice sharp. It was difficult to look directly up at her and lie to her face but Garnet knew there was nothing else she could do.

'Myrena was delivered of a still-born daughter,' she said softly, and Zeyd's nostrils flared.

'Ayb! My brother has failed again,' she said, her eyes dark. 'But at least there was a child, some fruit from the union.' Her shoulders drooped and it was as though she was talking not to Garnet but to herself.

'More than half a year has passed since he make a healthy girl, something must be done.' She stared at Garnet. 'You, come with us, beg sun god to smile on us, your prayers may be heard.'

Zeyd raised her jambiel to the skies, calling her warriors to order. They formed orderly ranks as the drummers at the rear began to beat out a rhythm.

Hirfa and her lover were goaded forward by the point of Zeyd's jambiel and they stumbled towards the hill top beyond the waterfall.

The hill was golden, bathed with light, as the snake-like ranks of women marched towards the crest. Garnet, glancing over her shoulder, was thankful that the path she trod was in the opposite direction to the one she had climbed earlier with Myrena in order to conceal her son.

Above her head gleamed a circle of copper that cast shimmering rays of red gold over the surrounding rocks. Kneeling before it, arms upraised, was Kabel, clad in a robe of black silk, a helmet of human bones resting on his hair. Beads of moisture stood out on his brow; there was not a patch of shade where he could shelter from the sun.

He rose when Zeyd went to him, resting her hand on his arm, speaking to him in English so that her warriors would not understand.

'You have failed yet again, my brother,' she said. 'The child Myrena carried was indeed a girl but it was still-born. You're strength has vanished, the fruits of your loins fall to the ground like barren seed. You must be replaced.'

He stared at her, his face drawn. 'I have prayed for hours on my knees to the sun god,' he said. 'I beg for one more chance to show my power. I shall take the white woman at the hour of El Assr, the time of the third prayer. Do you agree?'

Garnet held her breath in fear. Zeyd must refuse her brother's request and yet she hesitated. At last, she nodded.

'Very well, it shall be so. But now, we offer up Hirfa and the man in propition to the gods. Let us pray they will look on us with compassion.' She rested her hand on her brother's cheek for a moment. 'We are of the same blood. I do not wish your death on my hands.'

Zeyd addressed her warriors. She lifted her arms to the sky and began to chant. The drums beat out a soft, insistent rhythm. The sacrifice was about to begin.

Hirfa and her lover were tied with leather thongs to the large circle of copper. A wide band of goat skin was placed around the neck of each of them and Zeyd stepped forward, a girby of water in her hands. Slowly, she allowed the water to trickle over the leather bonds, turning them to a dark brown.

Hirfa began to struggle, the water running between her breasts, her eyes large with fear. The man at her side seemed devoid of resistance; his head touched his chest and his thin shoulders slumped in an attitude of utter defeat.

The women fell to the ground, heads bent as they began to intone strange words. Self-consciously, Garnet knelt down but she could not take her eyes from the two figures held against the copper circle that drew the sun's rays unmercifully.

She saw that, slowly, the leather was drying, growing tighter as the thongs hardened. When the sun reached its height, the life would be choked out of the unfortunate victims of the warriors' vengeance.

'Zeyd,' Garnet whispered. 'Could you not show mercy? They have surely suffered enough.'

'Silence.' The tribe leader looked down sternly. 'There is nothing to be done. The sun god must be appeased or we will all suffer.'

Led by Zeyd, the women slowly left the heat of the rocks and returned to the stillness of the village that slept in the afternoon sun. The water from the oasis shimmered under a haze and small insects called in the soft grass that grew beneath the shade of the covering hills.

Alone, Garnet sat in her tent. She had been unable to visit Wolfe. She had taken him no food that day and she had no way of knowing how long his supply of water would last.

She lay on her eskim. There was nothing to be done until night. Then she would visit him and try to coax him to eat some of the meat she had saved for him. They must get away from the village as soon as possible, for both their sakes.

*　　*　　*

The light was forming a pattern over his head. He saw skins sewn together to make a covering over his head and knew he was in a tent. He tried to sit up but the pain in his head was intense. He rested a moment and looked cautiously to his side. He saw a bulging girby and, carefully, he reached out for it, holding it to his lips with shaking hands, spilling some of the crystal water onto his face.

He moved over onto his side and stared towards the entrance where the dazzling sun threw a conical patch of light that pointed towards him like a long finger. He could make no sense of any of it.

He lifted his hand to the side of his head and felt the bandage. He had been wounded but could remember nothing of what had happened. He thought of the girl then, offering him food and water, her small white face crumpled as though she was about to cry. He could feel the softness of her hair as it touched his cheek. He felt he should know her name but it eluded him.

A shadow fell over the bright splash of sunlight and an old woman entered the tent, looking down at him with pebble-dark eyes. She spoke some words that meant nothing to him and scurried away as though she was frightened of him.

He lay back on the soft mat and closed his eyes. He was very tired and he wanted nothing more than to sleep. But it was not to be. A hand touched his cheek and, as, with an effort, he opened his eyes, he saw a beautiful woman staring down at him. Her breasts were bare and her golden hair half covered the gleaming brown skin. Her eyes were blue and smiling now as they looked into his.

'You have recovered, white one,' she said gently. 'It is a sign from the gods.' She turned and spoke to the old one who stood behind her. She was lifting his head then, cradling it on her strong bare thighs, smiling as she touched his lips with her fingertips.

She fed him hot, nourishing soup that was rich with meat. He could eat only a little but he felt some strength returning to his weakened body.

'What is your name, white one?' she asked, and he frowned, trying to clear his mind.

'I cannot remember,' he said at last. She put her head on one side, her eyes wondering.

'You do not remember who struck you down?' she asked, and he closed his eyes wearily.

'No. I remember nothing except waking up in this tent.' That was not quite true. There was the vision of a small face surrounded by lustrous red-gold hair but perhaps that was just a dream.

'I will have you removed to my tent,' she said to him. 'There I will nurse you back to health. I am Zeyd, leader of the warriors of the valley and I shall make you my king.'

He closed his eyes, his head ached and his vision was becoming blurred. He wanted only to rest but he was lifted onto a pallet of wood and being carried under the heat of the sun which glared down at him from a bowl of cloudless blue.

He was aware of his wound being washed and he felt the cold of wet, coarse leaves covering his brow. He was on a soft, comfortable bed and beside him sat the golden brown beauty with the long hair. She held his hand, talking to him softly, but he was too weary to hear. His eyes closed and he slept.

CHAPTER NINE

Garnet could not believe her eyes when she found the tent empty. The girby she had given Wolfe was still lying on the ground and alongside it was the blood-stained cloth from around his head.

'Wolfe!' Garnet placed her hand over her mouth, dread draining her body of strength. Was he worse, dead even? But that was a possibility she would not even consider.

She returned to her tent and lay in the darkness, unable to think or even to cry. He had become strangely dear to her as she had nursed him back to health. Cradling him in her arms, she had experienced an undefinable tenderness, a wish to protect him from harm. And now she did not even know what had become of him.

When the morning sun pointed fingers of light into her tent, she rose from her eskim, unrefreshed. Her eyes ached with unshed tears and she felt a numbing despair close around her.

Her tent flap was flung open and Myrena was smiling at her. She still wore the long robe that covered her entirely and she crouched down on the eskim, her arms folded around her body.

'I have succoured my child,' she said happily. 'He will be strong man one day.' Her face fell. 'Soon, I must make plan for you to take him away from valley.'

She stared at Garnet's white face, her head on one side.

'But there is something wrong, tell me.' She placed her hand on Garnet's arm, drawing down on the eskim beside her.

'It's Wolfe, the white man, where is he, Myrena?' She clasped her hands together, her heart beating swiftly and she saw the queen frown.

'He is well, Zeyd, she take him, look after him even though Kabel greatly angry.' She shrugged. 'I worry about my king. I do not wish to lose him.'

Garnet felt weak with relief. She closed her eyes, her hands over her face, her thoughts spinning like leaves tossed in the wind. Wolfe was safe and for the moment that was all that mattered.

She became aware then of Myrena's sadness. The queen loved Kabel, it was in her eyes, and now she was anxious about his fate.

'What will happen to Kabel if he is no longer king?' she asked, and she saw the other woman's eyes widen.

'In my youth, the old king die and then there is new one,' she said. 'Since then there has only been Kabel. If he cast aside perhaps he die too.'

Garnet bit her lip. 'But Zeyd is his sister. Surely she will not allow anything to happen to him?'

Myrena rose to her feet. 'I do not know the answer.'

Her face was turned away from Garnet. 'I cannot lose my son and my king.'

She left quickly, her footsteps whispering over the grass, her long robe fluttering behind her. Garnet sighed, she would never become accustomed to the ways of these strange people. But at least she knew now that Wolfe was safe.

She felt a sudden sense of excitement. Now that Zeyd was personally interested in Wolfe's welfare, it would not be long before he would be well enough to leave the valley with her. Together they could take Myrena's son to the safety of Jonathon's house. The child was after all his grandson and would be welcomed in the Summers' residence with open arms.

When Zeyd sent for her a short time later, Garnet forced herself to be calm. She must not show by so much as a flicker of her eyelashes that she was eager to speak to Wolfe alone.

The tribe leader was kneeling on the ground outside her tent, painting her arms with brightly coloured designs. Her long hair was loose and well combed, hanging softly on her naked shoulders.

'The man.' She jerked her head towards the tent. 'I wish you to care for him. He is a little stronger now and in two passes of the moon, he be bound to me.'

Garnet stared at Zeyd. 'I don't understand,' she said quietly. 'Do you mean to make him king?'

The woman's eyes were shrewd. 'Do not worry,' she said. 'I will not turn Kabel out, not just yet. You will have your chance with him, it will be a test for both of you. If there is failure to produce a girl then . . .' She shrugged. 'My brother must die.'

She rose to her feet. 'But before then, I shall see if the white man can do any better. I shall be his woman.' She smiled. 'We shall enter into a contest, see who it is brings girl child to tribe.'

Garnet entered Zeyd's tent and found it was almost as large and luxurious as her brothers. Her bed was less imposing but was nevertheless a well-made structure of wood raised on bulbous legs and covered with a bright eskim of red and gold.

Then she saw Wolfe. He was standing watching her with unnerving intensity. He looked pale but was obviously much stronger than when she'd seen him last. She moved closer to him.

'Wolfe, I'm so glad . . .' Her words broke off in mid-sentence. There was no recognition in his silver-grey eyes. He shook his head as though trying to clear his thoughts.

'You call me Wolfe and speak as though you know me but I have never seen you before.'

Garnet felt as though he'd struck her. 'Wolfe, you are still not fully recovered, perhaps you should be resting.' She longed to go to him, to cradle his head against her, but he was suddenly a stranger and she could not approach him.

'We could not have been important to each other,' he said softly, almost as though talking to himself. The words of protest died on Garnet's lips as Zeyd stepped into the tent. Wolfe had eyes for no one then but the statuesque tribe leader.

Zeyd went to Wolfe, resting her hand against his

shoulder in an uncharacteristic show of gentleness.

'The maiden shall serve you with meat so that you grow strong. Together we must build up my tribe of warriors, their future lies with us, my love.'

Zeyd settled herself on the carpeted floor, before a low table, and began to eat her meal, plucking at the meat with long slim fingers. She watched with narrowed eyes as Garnet handed Wolfe a platter of meat and rice, obviously impatient for her to leave them alone.

In her own tent once more, Garnet sank onto her eskim, fighting the feeling of panic that was rising within her. The threat of marriage to Kabel hung over her and yet how could she leave the valley with Wolfe sick in mind if not in body?

Perhaps if she told him all that had happened, how Zeyd had callously struck him down, his mind would clear. But perhaps he would simply refuse to believe her. He had treated her like a stranger and when Zeyd had entered the tent, his eyes had lit with an inner glow as though he was bewitched by her.

The next morning, just as the sun was rising, Zeyd sent for Garnet. The tribe leader was outside her tent, combing her long hair.

'I wish you to attend my man,' she said. 'Today we will be bound together by tribal laws. I wish you to go to him, prepare him for me, oil his body and anoint him with herbs of fertility so that our union shall bear fruit.' Her smile was cruel as she saw Garnet's stricken face.

'I see you want my man for yourself but that cannot

be. You are my brother's chosen one.' She made an impatient gesture with her hands. 'Go, obey my commands.'

Garnet moved within the tent and saw Wolfe sitting, utterly relaxed, on the brightly coloured eskim. He rose to his feet, staring down, waiting with cold politeness for her to speak.

'I have to prepare you for your wedding with the tribe leader.' Garnet was very conscious of Zeyd standing just outside the tent. She drew closer to Wolfe, uncertain how she was supposed to perform her task.

'Take the oil.' He spoke as though she was a stranger. 'It is to be rubbed into my body.' He disrobed quickly and stood before her waiting, an expression of impatience crossing his face.

She rubbed his shoulders; they were broad, tanned by the sun. She suddenly longed to hold him close, to feel his arms wind around her waist, his hands caressing and gentle.

'Wolfe, do you not remember anything?' she whispered urgently. 'There is danger for us if we remain. We must leave the valley as soon as possible.'

He looked at her with sympathy. 'Do not concern yourself.' He spoke soothingly. 'You are in no danger.' He turned to allow her to smooth the oil into his chest and abdomen. 'Zeyd has told me about your strange notions. They come only from too much sun. You are to be bride to the king of the tribe. Where is the peril in that?'

Garnet ceased to rub oil into his long lean body and

bit her lip in consternation. Zeyd had been more cunning than she had anticipated.

Garnet's hands moved downwards. 'Do you not remember holding me in your arms, Wolfe, and making love to me?' she asked desperately.

Before he could answer, Zeyd was inside the tent, her long hair hanging over her naked breasts, her head high as she stood hands on hips, watching Garnet.

'That is enough,' she said in her harsh voice. 'The Hakim comes to say his spells over us.' She smiled up at Wolfe and he rested his hand on her shoulder. Garnet made to leave them but Zeyd's next words stopped her.

'Remain with us,' she said. 'You shall serve us with meat and drink later.'

The tent flap opened and a bizarre figure stepped inside. The garments were of flame and black, the headpiece a skull. The face was covered in a variety of coloured chalks but, nonetheless, Garnet recognized Kabel's strong features beneath the paint.

He held out his long arms, encompassing Zeyd and Wolfe and he began to intone a strange chant. From his belt, he took a pouch and a heavy perfume filled the air as he swung it from side to side.

He held a cup to Zeyd's lips and, laughing, she pushed it aside.

'I am not one of your brides. I do not need chine to dull my senses, my brother.'

He moved back at last and bowed his head and Zeyd took Wolfe's hand in hers.

'We may go now to the waterfall and complete our

joining,' she said softly, her eyes bright.

Garnet prayed that Wolfe would recover his memory in time to stop the strange marriage going any further. But to her dismay, he went willingly with Zeyd, his hand caressing her arm.

Kabel turned to her. 'You stay, wait for Zeyd's return and serve her with whatever food she requires.' He stepped nearer to her, his hand cupping her chin.

'Do not look so dispirited. Our marriage draws near and this time I shall not fail. I shall give you my daughter and prove to the tribe that I am fit to rule as their king. This white man, this usurper, he will have to be dealt with when the right time comes.'

He left her and Garnet sank down onto her knees, her eyes dry, though she longed to cry out her fears. She was torn in two. Should she leave while she could with Myrena's new-born son? If she delayed even by a day or two, it might be too late.

And yet how could she leave Wolfe, helpless and unsuspecting as he was? In spite of feeling she had been betrayed by him, she knew she could not desert him; she would have to try once more to make him remember what had happened to them both.

It was over an hour later that Zeyd returned leading Wolfe into her tent, an expression of triumph on her face. Their naked bodies gleamed with water and Wolfe's hair hung close to his forehead.

'Bring us food.' Zeyd stretched out across the bed and stared at Garnet. 'We are both very hungry.' She smiled and touched Wolfe's cheek as he sat beside her, drawing on a long robe of white cotton.

'We shall prove that you are more of a king than my brother ever could be,' she said with satisfaction. 'Together, we shall make a strong tribe of warriors, more powerful than any other.'

Garnet slipped out of the tent and helped herself to a platter of meat from the long table spread for the evening meal. The rice was fluffy, mixed with aromatic herbs and a scattering of raisins. The food smelled tempting but Garnet was not hungry. She saw Myrena beckoning to her.

'You have lost the white man to Zeyd,' she whispered. 'He will never leave valley now. Come to me at the foot of the mountain path at moonlight if you wish to go, for tomorrow at El Assr is your wedding with Kabel.'

A smile curved her mouth even though her eyes were moist. 'I have named my boy. Tell Jonathon Summers that he is to be called Tassili like the rocks of the desert.'

Garnet stood staring at the queen, unable to sort out the confusion of her thoughts. Only one thing was clear: she could not stay and be married to Kabel.

'I will come with you tonight,' she whispered to Myrena. 'I must go now and take this food to Zeyd.' She hurried across the grassy land, her thoughts in a turmoil. Should she make one last plea to Wolfe to come with her?

He was alone in the tent. His gaze met Garnet's and he frowned, a puzzled expression clouding the greyness of his eyes. He held out a hand towards her and she took it, her fingers curling in his.

'Wolfe,' she said. 'Please try to remember.' She stood on tiptoe and pressed her lips to his. He slowly took her in his arms, holding her close and, breathlessly, she broke away, willing him to recapture the memories that seemed lost to him.

He moved away from her, his hand to his head. The wound was healed now, leaving only a thin red scar across his temple. He turned and stared at her, an anguished look in his eyes.

'I seem to recall traces of the past,' he said frowning. 'I remember a ship on fire, the water gleaming redly.' He paused and thumped his fist into the palm of his other hand in frustration.

'It's gone, what's the use of trying?' He turned as though he was about to say more, then his eyes looked past her to where Zeyd was entering at the door.

'You have brought food,' she said to Garnet. 'It took you long enough. Serve us and then go.'

She reclined on the bed, staring at Wolfe and Garnet with half-closed eyes.

'What have you been talking about?' she challenged. 'Have you been wondering in your mind again, white woman?'

Garnet bit back a sharp retort. Zeyd was enough of an enemy without antagonizing her further. She placed the food in bowls and, with a bow, left the tent. Her spirits were rising. It seemed that, at last, Wolfe was beginning to remember, but would it be in time for him to make his escape with her tonight? It was only the faintest possibility but at least now she felt some sense of purpose and hope.

She waited impatiently for the sun to slip through the orange and gold haze of the sky and disappear behind the hills. The inky blackness brought with it a chill wind and Garnet wrapped herself in a cloak of skins and stood at the doorway of her tent waiting for the moon to silver the grass.

Hardly daring to breathe, she crossed the open land, trying to keep as low as possible, using the shadows thrown by the tents as cover. She crept on all fours inside the sleeping place where Zeyd lay alongside Wolfe, her arm flung across his broad chest.

Garnet stared down at them for a moment and closed her eyes in despair. It was clear that she would not be able to awaken Wolfe without disturbing Zeyd too.

'Forgive me,' she murmured, and sped on reckless feet, back through the moonlight.

In an agony of indecision, she stopped running, staring round her like a trapped animal. But she had to go on. If she stayed, she would be married to Kabel and she would never be allowed any freedom. This was her one opportunity of making her escape. She would be foolish to put it aside and for a man who never professed to care about her.

She forced herself to go towards the path leading up into the hillside. She would take the baby and make her way to Jonathon Summers. Then perhaps he would make the decision concerning Wolfe's release from the valley.

But the pathway remained empty. Garnet waited, crouched between the rocks, eyes straining to see across the camp, until, at last, the morning light streaked the sky. She knew then that Myrena was not coming.

Reluctantly, she walked back down the slope towards the still-sleeping camp. The oasis shimmered greyly under the overhanging rocks and the waterfall tumbled downwards, the spray silver in the dawn.

It was Kabel himself who came to her tent with the news. He stood, arms folded over his gigantic chest, his long hair glowing in the sunshine.

'The queen is sick,' he said. 'She lies in her bed and she wishes to speak with you.' He held up his hand as Garnet would have moved to leave him.

'Wait. The joining between us takes place at El Assr, just after noon. The women will come to prepare you in just a few minutes. You must see my queen later.' He shrugged. 'There is no hurry, you can do nothing for her that the sisters cannot do.'

He smiled. 'I look forward to being together with you under the waters of the mountains. I will be sure that I fill you with my child.'

He strode away from her and Garnet looked around her desperately. She must run and hide somewhere, anywhere, until she could see Myrena and get her to point the way through the mountains.

She stepped forward but she was too late. She could see the women coming towards her, carrying chalks and a bowl of water. Worse, one of them carried a cup, and with a sinking sensation Garnet realized that she would be given chine. Her senses would grow dull, her will would leave her, she would be nothing more than a lifeless doll to be bent to Kabel's will.

CHAPTER TEN

The chine tasted like honey, thick and sweet, but with a bitterness that caught Garnet's breath. She coughed and one of the women smiled, but with gentle pressure forced her to drink to the bottom of the cup.

The paints were bright, forming intricate patterns on her white skin. The colours wavered before Garnet's eyes and she realized the chine was taking effect. But somehow there was no sense of panic, already she was becoming resigned.

Her eyes were painted with kahl, her brows darkened with chalk. The women talked softly, laughing, admiring their own handiwork, and Garnet began to relax against the cushions placed behind her head.

She was floating in a dream world where nothing seemed to be real. Her hands were too large as she watched the nails turning from pearl to scarlet. She was urged to rise to her feet and she did so with no effort. One moment she was lying on her eskim, the next she was on her feet; there was no sensation of movement. Patterns were made along the flat planes of her stomach and Garnet stared at them, fascinated, as they seemed to pulsate with life. Her hair was combed and flowers woven into the long strands and she was ready.

The throb of drums was inside her head as she was led forward. The soft silk of a robe whispered over her shoulders in a fall of scarlet and gold and black, tumbling around her bare feet. The sun was very bright now, throwing patterns of light and shade onto the ground. Garnet walked forward with measured tread, making her way towards the awning.

Kabel was waiting for her. He seemed taller than ever, gigantic and beautiful with an oriel of gold around his head. He smiled and took her hand and before them stood the Hakim who was Zeyd now and words were spoken that fluttered around her mind like butterflies.

Young girls, arms full of flowers, danced to the beat of the drums. The blooms were extended towards Garnet and then drawn back and the brilliant colours of oleander spun round in her line of vision.

The cloak was removed from her and she was conscious of the heat of the sun on her naked body. She was walking forward and yet her feet seemed not to touch the bright grass. The waterfall was before her, tumbling golden and studded with diamonds onto the flat rock below where she was being placed.

Water rippled beneath her body and fell like soft fingers against her skin. Above her was Kabel, his hair darkened now by water, his arms huge as they reached for her.

He was between her legs, his body roused and
eager. He spoke words to her but she could not hear
them for the music of the waterfall that washed pleasantly over her.

A part of her mind waited for Kabel to plunge and,
though she knew that pain would surely come, she did
not attempt to move. She could not, she was in-
capable of making any decision. She simply lay
waiting.

But he was rising up away from her, his face
darkened with anger. Beyond him was Wolfe, his eyes
fierce as he talked, his face intense.

She was drawn from the waterfall and she stood
quite still, watching the two men talk.

'She is not a maiden,' Wolfe was saying. 'I have lain
with the woman, she is mine and not worthy to be
Kabel's bride.'

The king lunged towards Wolfe, large hands reaching for his throat. Garnet realized dimly that the white
man would have no chance of defending himself
against the hugeness of Kabel. He had been greatly
weakened by his wounds and was still pale.

It was Zeyd who moved forward to stop her brother.
She spoke to him rapidly in his own language and he
stood back, his great shoulders heaving. He stared at
Garnet and then turned once more to Wolfe as though,
even yet, he might take the man's life. Zeyd spoke
again, more sharply, and he moved away, his large
head bent.

Myrena, her face wreathed in pain, a robe held
around her body, came forward from her tent. She

took Garnet's arm and led her away, speaking to her in soft words that fell like leaves in autumn around Garnet's ears.

She was lying on her own eskim then and she felt weary. Her head was beginning to ache and her eyes were closing. She was aware of nothing but the need to sleep and it was with gratitude that she saw Myrena place a cover over her nakedness.

The memories had flooded in as Wolfe had stood in the hot sunshine watching Garnet being led forward to her marriage with Kabel. He had been unable to trust his own thoughts at first, but then his mind had cleared and he realized that the woman at whose side he now stood had been his attacker. She had almost killed him with one blow of the blade that hung from her belt.

His eyes moved from Zeyd to Garnet. Her small face was expressionless, her eyes unblinking. It was apparent even from such a distance that some kind of potion had been administered to her.

He saw her taken beneath the waterfall and it was only when he saw the huge form of Kabel kneel before Garnet, ready to violate her tiny, defenceless body that something snapped.

Now Zeyd faced him, her lips drawn back from gleaming teeth, her eyes filled with anger and hatred.

'We fight to the death white man.' Her voice was an animal snarl. 'You break rules of tribe, you die.'

He stared back at her, his eyes challenging. 'Is it the tribe laws that worry you or the knowledge that I do not want you, not at any price?'

She threw a jambiel to him. The blade flashed in the sunlight and Zeyd began to circle him, her feet light on the grass, her body tensed, ready to spring. She was a strong woman, arms as big as any man's and Wolfe knew he would have to use cunning if he was to overpower her.

'Fight, dog!' she said harshly.

There was a clash of blades and Zeyd's magnificent body was close to Wolfe's as she struggled against him. He stepped away from her quickly and she spun round, her jambiel pointing at his throat.

'You will taste the edge of my sword before the sun rises much higher.' She panted, her hair swinging over her face, her eyes alight with venom.

She edged cautiously nearer to him, bent almost double, her long arms extended, her jambiel swinging towards his heart. She was forcing the pace, knowing he would shortly tire, and the urge to kill was almost tangible as she forced him backwards.

Waiting for the right moment, Wolfe avoided her sweeping blade. Then, so suddenly that she was taken completely off guard, he held his jambiel up to the light so that it reflected into Zeyd's eyes, blinding her.

He moved quickly, his foot behind her legs, his arm at her throat, tossing her backwards onto the ground. His blade was close to the pulse beating in her neck and she stared up at him, her eyes wide.

'I spare your life,' Wolfe said, throwing aside his jambiel. 'You will have to spare mine.'

She jumped to her feet, intent on rushing towards him, her eyes gleaming wickedly. A harsh voice stopped her and Wolfe saw the queen, standing regally in the doorway of Garnet's tent, her face pale, her hand clutching a robe around her body.

She spoke again and Zeyd fell back uncertainly. Wolfe could not understand what was being said, but he guessed that Myrena was upholding the laws of her tribe and defying Zeyd to go against them.

Zeyd issued a command to her warriors and Wolfe found himself being bound by strong cords, his wrists secured behind his back. A dark hood was pulled over his head and he was pushed forward, stumbling over the uneven ground.

He felt the land grow stony, sloping upwards, and he knew they must be treading the pathway between the mountains. He could scarcely breathe beneath the folds of the suffocating cloth and the heat was intense as the sun beat mercilessly down on him.

They walked for what seemed a long time. His senses grew numb and the motion of his legs was instinctive. He felt a sense of thirst and realized by the heat and softness under his feet that he was walking in desert country. At last, the cloth was removed from his face and a warrior cut the cords that bound his hands.

Zeyd stared at him, her head raised, her eyes hostile.

'I am bound by the laws of my tribe not to kill you,' she said. Her hand gestured to the sun-baked terrain. 'I expect my land to do the work for me.'

Fleet of foot, as though fresh from their beds, the warriors retreated across the sand. Wolfe watched them disappear over a ridge and he was alone without food or water under the merciless heat of the African sun. He sank to his knees, trying to conserve his energy. But he knew he must find shade and moisture or, before many hours passed, he would be dead. He stared up at the blinding sun and with an effort pulled himself to his feet. He must somehow return to civilization and find help. He could not leave Garnet to face alone the anger of Zeyd and her warriors.

Garnet awoke slowly. Sensations were returning to her extremities and the strange ache had disappeared from her brow. Her thoughts were crystal clear as she remembered Wolfe's intervention at her marriage to Kabel. He had stepped forward just in time to save her, but what had become of him? She sat up and saw she was in her own tent. She realized it was very early in the morning and the birds were singing outside in the acacia trees. That meant she had slept for hours. It had been just after noon when the ceremony was interrupted so the entire afternoon and night had passed since she fell asleep.

Myrena entered the tent, her eyes were full of compassion. She took Garnet's arm and raised her to her feet. She did not look at her; it was as though she was ashamed to meet Garnet's eyes.

'What's going to happen?' Garnet asked, her voice trembling, and, sadly, Myrena shook her head. She did not speak but led Garnet to where the entire tribe of women were gathered in the clearing. The warriors stood at the forefront and, behind them, the nursing mothers, pitifully few, clearly demonstrating Kabel's failing powers. At the rear were the old ones, the elders of the tribe, in hoods and white robes with dark eyes staring at her with curiosity.

Zeyd caught her wrists and bound them, jerking her arms above her head and securing Garnet to a crossed piece of wood. She, stepped away from her, a triumphant smile on her face.

'You will be flogged,' she said. 'And then offered as a sacrifice to the sun gods. Think of this, your lover lies out in the desert land. He too will die as surely as if my jambiel had pierced his heart.'

Kabel stood before her then, a coiled whip in his strong hand, a look of hatred in his eyes. The drums began to beat and he drew back his arm, the muscles rippling under bronzed skin. The whip descended and, for a moment, Garnet felt nothing.

The stinging pain was like fire, snaking around her body, across her stomach and up to her breasts. She pulled against her bonds, trying desperately to free herself, but she was tied expertly and the cords would not be loosened.

The whip fell around her feet and, with slow cruelty, Kabel wound it around his elbow and forearm, preparing himself to strike again.

'If you beg for mercy, perhaps my brother will stop,' Zeyd suggested, her eyes alight. Garnet shook her head; she knew nothing would deter Kabel from his act of revenge.

The whip cracked against the still air, even the drums had stopped beating. It was as though the whole world waited for the slap as the cord struck bare flesh.

Garnet jerked forward, moaning softly, her lips sore where her teeth bit into them in an effort to stop the screams that rose to her throat. She felt blood trickle down her back, between her buttocks, and a long line of red appeared across her breasts.

At last, her wracked body could stand no more pain and a darkness closed in on her as she hung limply from her bonds. She felt hands releasing her and heard Myrena's softly whispered encouragement and then she was drifting on a dark stream that dragged her into its murky depths.

She became conscious briefly to find Myrena rubbing oils and herbs into her bruised and broken skin. The queen smiled reassuringly, holding a girby to her lips. The water was sweet and clear and Garnet tried to thank Myrena but the words would not come. She closed her eyes and slept.

Her mind was clear when she woke again. She struggled to sit up, wincing a little, her body aching and sore. Myrena brought her a bowl of mutton stew and fed her as though she were a child.

'Grow strong,' she said softly. 'For sake of my baby.' She fell silent as Zeyd entered the tent and stood staring down at Garnet in contempt.

'My queen wastes her time nourishing you for, tomorrow, you will meet your death on the circle of copper.' She stared at Myrena, head high.

'My brother too must die. He is no longer man enough to rule.' No one spoke for a long moment and Zeyd turned on her heels, moving towards the entrance.

'I shall choose a new king when the time is right and you, Myrena, will be put among the old ones, your days as queen are over. The tribe is all mine now, do you understand?'

As Myrena remained silent, Zeyd spoke to her quickly in her own language. She left the tent, a triumphant smile on her lips, and the queen sank down onto her knees, her arms around her body. She seemed to be praying and, when at last she rose to her feet, she was calm. She left Garnet alone with her own thoughts. She felt again the softness of Wolfe's hair against her cheek and the thought of him out there in the desert was almost too much to bear.

She shivered then as she thought of her own fate. She could not rid her mind of the picture of Hirfa pinioned against the gleaming copper circle, slowly being choked to death under the merciless sun. She covered her face with her hands but her eyes were without tears. Her pain and bitterness went too deep for the shallow relief of crying.

CHAPTER ELEVEN

The craggy rocks cast long black shadows in stark relief against the rippling, endless sand. With a sigh of relief, Wolfe crawled into the coolness, closing his eyes against the sensation of burning blindness. Several miles back, he had found an acacia tree and had stripped the shallow roots from the sand, sucking at the previous drops of moisture contained inside. But now his body cried out for water, his lips were cracked and dry, his body weakened by the effort of walking through the fine, clinging whiteness of the desert sand. It was only the thought of Garnet's danger that drove him on to greater efforts. If he did not return to the valley with help, and soon, she would be sacrificed by the power-crazed leader of the warrior women.

The sun was lower now and soon the cold of night would sweep over the desert lands. Wolfe believed he would make better progress in the darkness; he should reach the home of his partner Summers by early morning if his calculations were correct.

The image of Garnet's white face and tiny, perfect body invaded his mind. She had saved his life when he

lay in the valley of women, dying from lack of care. She
had brought him food and water and shown him great
tenderness.

He pushed the thoughts away, he must not allow his
emotions, his feelings of gratitude to cloud his judgement. That was a path he had trodden before with
Lucia, to his cost.

The dark shadows were lengthening around the
rocks where he lay and Wolfe pushed himself to his
feet, forcing himself to begin walking towards the face
of the dying sun. His eyes were stinging so that he
could hardly see and he knew that, once the dazzling
white of the sand faded into moonlit silver, his vision
would be worse. It was nothing that a wash in clear
water and a good night's sleep would not cure but, at
this moment, he needed all his senses, alert and aware,
or he could easily become lost in the vast tracts of
desert.

A fennec fox ran past him and Wolfe moved on more
quickly, following the creature's tracks as far as he
could. He realized there must be water nearby, but
once the wind shifted, the animal's footprints would
vanish.

He came upon the oasis quite suddenly, stumbling
into the coarse grass that surrounded the shining
water. He sank down, plunging his head into the cool
stillness, allowing the water to trickle into his mouth.
He took care not to drink too much at once. He would
rest a while and take small amounts of liquid at inter-
vals, and then, when the night was at its coldest, he
would go on. He knew he was gradually losing his

strength and his mind told him that he could not walk for many more miles and yet, when he thought of Garnet, he was possessed by a fierce determination not to fail her. He looked up at the night sky and the vision of her pale face, surrounded by a tangle of red-gold hair, rose up before him. Tiredly, he stumbled to his feet and began to walk away from the life-giving waters of the oasis.

The women of the village were stirring from their beds, the birds calling their raucous songs to the morning. Garnet opened her eyes and knew this was the day of her execution.

She rose from her eskim and drank a little of the water Myrena had left for her the previous night. She was still bruised and sore from her beating at the hands of Kabel and yet she could feel it within her to be sorry for him because he, too, would suffer at Zeyd's hands.

The guards arrived for her early. The two enormous women were dressed in full battle attire. Breastplates of copper gleamed against bronzed skin and skirts of copper circles clinked as the women walked. Garnet offered no resistance. What was the use? Gripped by strong hands, she was forced from her tent out into the sweet morning air.

Zeyd was standing before her group of warriors. Her hair was braided into tiny plaits decorated with coloured beads. She was magnificent in the pale sunshine, her skin gleaming, her hair bright as the sun itself.

'You will die slowly, this I promise you, white one,' she said in a low voice. She turned away, the copper circles of her skirt moving gently, flashing points of light from a myriad surfaces.

As the drums began to beat a slow, sinister rhythm, the guards pushed Garnet forward towards the dark outline of the craggy hills. The sun was rising higher in the sky, the heat already intense. Garnet could feel the grip of leather thongs around her wrists and knew that soon she would know the cruel roughness of the cord around her throat. But she would not show her fear; she was determined to defy Zeyd in spirit, if she could not do so in body.

The climb along the rocky path was slow and the sun blistered down, reflecting heat from the stark, bare mountainside. Garnet looked up and above her saw the shimmering circle of copper like a second sun against a cloudless sky. Her heart dipped in fear, but her steps did not falter.

When the plateau on the mountaintop was reached, Zeyd fell to her knees, her arms raised heavenward as she began to chant. The drums rolled and the guards took Garnet, pressing her against the heat of the copper disc, fastening her wrists and ankles securely.

Zeyd herself placed the thick collar of leather around Garnet's slender throat. She smiled slowly as she lifted the girby of water high, allowing the sparkling drops to soak into the leather.

'We shall leave you alone to the mercy of the sun gods,' she said. 'Take your time to die, white woman. I only wish I could watch but no one is allowed to see the spirit leave the body.'

The drums were beating faster now and the women hurried back along the path, uncomfortable in the noon heat. Garnet watched the snake-like line of warriors disappear over the brow of the hill and she was alone with nothing but the brilliant sun burning down upon her and the flat barren rocks beneath her feet. Already she felt breathless, beads of moisture covered her face. The noose was tightening around her neck.

In a sudden panic, she tried to move her head, the hide chaffed her skin and she began to cough. She became still, holding her head erect, allowing herself a small respite from the hardness of the collar.

She closed her eyes and moistened her dry lips. Soon there would be no escape, the leather would constrict her throat and she would die alone in an alien country. The heat of the copper behind her was like a fire. Moisture trickled between her breasts and along the flatness of her stomach. Her mouth was parched, tasting of salt, and she longed for a cooling drink of water.

There was a sound behind her. As if by a miracle, Myrena appeared, her sharp knife cutting into the cord that bound Garnet. Her face was strained and her lips were almost blue, but the queen was smiling as she supported Garnet against her shoulder.

'We must leave valley at once,' she said. 'Zeyd believe that Kabel take me out into desert to die as is our custom. When he not return, she think he perish too, she not care, she wish to be rid of him.' She held a girby to Garnet's dry lips. 'But she must not see us take you, come quickly.'

Skirting the valley, they arrived at the place where Tassili had been hidden. Seated beside the child was Kabel.

'We must go to the house of my father, Jonathon Summers,' he said. 'We take a risk bringing you, woman, but Myrena wish it.' He was silent for a moment, aware of his queen's disapproving look. He shrugged. 'I wish it too. You have been kind to Myrena and we owe you a debt.'

He picked up a large pack of clothes and food and led the way from the cave along the narrow path. Myrena took her son and wrapped him in a length of cotton, binding him to her own body, leaving her hands free.

In the rear came Garnet, dressed now in a long cotton robe. Myrena, it seemed, had thought very carefully about the plan of escape. That it had all been the queen's idea was clear to Garnet, Kabel had not the wit to provide so adequately for the journey ahead.

They descended from the valley mouth into a deep cavern of rocks with sandy soil lined with rows of cypress trees. Here, Myrena sank to her knees and began to feed her child. Garnet sat beside her, watching anxiously, noting the dark shadows beneath the woman's eyes and the high colour that burned in her cheeks.

Garnet placed her palm against the queen's forehead. It was burning. Their eyes met and Myrena shook her head, warning Garnet to say nothing. She was very sick but such was the woman's strength that, when Kabel began to move on, she rose to her feet and followed him without demur.

Garnet stumbled along behind, her body aching, her mind dulled by the merciless heat. Around her throat was traced a harsh red mark where the leather had begun to burn into her skin. She did not know how much longer she could go on and yet she was reluctant to call a halt, knowing that if Zeyd discovered what had happened, her vengeance would be swift and final.

At last, it was Myrena who weakened. She fell onto her side, her eyes alight with fever, her lips trembling. Garnet knelt quickly beside her and placed her hand beneath the queen's head.

'I must feed baby,' Myrena said urgently, and Garnet, after a moment, nodded. She helped unwind the infant and held him to his mother's breast. He gurgled and sucked with vigour and a glimmer of a smile touched Myrena's mouth.

'Let him drink well,' she said softly, and Garnet felt a lump rise to her throat Sick as she was, the queen's first thought was for her child.

Garnet spoke quietly to Kabel. 'She is too weak to go on,' she said. 'We shall have to rest here under the trees where there is a little shade.'

Kabel looked down at his wife. 'What evil spirit has entered her?' he asked, clearly distraught at the rapid deterioration of his wife's condition.

'I believe she has child-bed sickness,' Garnet said gently. 'Let her rest for a while and we shall see how she feels when she has slept and eaten.'

Kabel arranged a shelter of cloth drawn across two tree branches while Garnet took some rice and held it to Myrena's lips. She shook her head, her eyes dark.

'Do not waste good food,' she said simply. 'You, take care of baby, give him water when he cries.' Her voice was failing. She nodded as Garnet wrapped the boy against her own body, feeling his soft weight against her breasts.

Myrena lifted her arm with an effort and made a sign over her son's forehead in blessing. His small hand reached out, his fingers curling in those of his mother, and she smiled.

'My son meant for greatness,' she said. 'Take care of him and of his father.'

She lay back, panting in distress, her face a mask of pain. Garnet stared up at Kabel in helpless appeal and he knelt beside his wife.

He spoke to her in his own language, his arm beneath her shoulder. She gave a little cry and shook her head and he lowered her once more to the ground.

'I would carry her,' he said to Garnet. 'But it brings too much pain.'

There was a deep silence as though a waiting hush had fallen on the place where they sat. Only the harsh, rasping sound of Myrena's laboured breathing disturbed the stillness.

Biting her lip, Garnet stared down at the once-proud, strong queen. Her hair was tangled over her face and her flesh had shrunk from the large bones of her face. She was ravaged by fever, her mind wandering now, her open eyes seeing what no one else could.

She gave a long sigh like the wind in the branches of the trees and her head fell sideways.

Kabel rose to his feet, his great shoulders slumped, his long arms hanging at his sides.

'Her spirit has departed,' he said. 'She is gone from us.'

Overhead, a raven called harshly on the hot still air and the sound shook Kabel into movement.

'Go on, white one,' he said to Garnet. 'I stay to bury my dead.' He knelt and began to dig a shallow grave with his bare hands and Garnet felt tears choke her throat.

'I'll wait for you,' she said thickly, and Kabel turned to look at her, pausing for a moment in his task of moving the dry earth.

'Go, take my son to safety. Zeyd might even now be following our trail.'

Garnet pushed herself to her feet, the baby heavy in her arms. Kabel was right. Her legs were trembling as she took a step forward.

'Take the line of cypress trees as your guide,' Kabel said. 'Soon, you will come to the Rio Hut and you must follow the waters of the river for several hours. By sunset, you will see the house of my father, Jonathon Summers, and you will be safe.'

His eyes met hers. 'I will follow when I can, but I ask your forgiveness for my harshness now. Do you give it?'

Garnet nodded. 'Yes,' she said simply. She saw him resume his digging and knew there was nothing more for them to say to each other. She looked up at the tree tops and forced herself to walk steadily over the dry soil. She would not weep for Myrena; she would channel her strength into the arduous task before her.

When at last the silver of the Rio Hut came into view, Garnet breathed a sigh of relief. She sank down onto her knees in the shelter of a group of shrubs, hearing, with a sense of joy, the musical sound of the water rushing past her.

Tassili nestled close, his breath sweet upon her cheek. He slept peacefully, still content, not yet troubled by the pangs of hunger that must surely come. Garnet lay her head on the dusty ground and closed her eyes and slept.

When she awoke, the baby's eyes were open and they were so like his mother's that Garnet felt a pain inside her. She took a little water from the girby and moistened the infant's small mouth and he sucked obediently, with no complaint.

She became aware that the sky was darkening although the sun was still at its height. There came a long whine of the wind rising like a song, and dust flew into Garnet's face. She stumbled to her feet, knowing she must seek shelter before the storm broke over her. She held Tassili's small face close to her breast and he began to cry as though sensing danger.

Garnet had lost sight of the river and in her panic ran blindly forward. Her searching hand found the hardness of rock and, with a small cry, she crouched under a ledge, sheltered by an enormous boulder.

It was pitch black now, without even a glimmer of light, and Garnet felt the stinging cut of the sand as it grazed the soft skin from her ankle that jutted from the small cave where she crouched. She wrapped the baby closer to her, his hair beneath her chin, and she was afraid.

The wind abated at last and Garnet stretched her stiff limbs. With an effort, she got to her feet and stared round her in awe, the landscape was completely changed. She was totally lost.

CHAPTER TWELVE

Wolfe stood in the window of Jonathon Summers' sitting room staring out at the fierce desert storm raging through the flatlands, battering the old timbers of the building as though to crush it to the ground. He was in a fever of impatience to be on a horse riding back to the valley of women in search of Garnet. But the storm was his enemy.

He realized how fortunate he had been in finding his way out of the desert in time to avoid being caught in the howling wind and flying sand. His long experience had come to his aid. He had followed the instincts born of practical knowledge and, once he had come upon familiar landmarks, it had only been a short time before he reached safety.

'You seem well rested, my boy.' Jonathon moved up behind him, staring out at the dusty scene before him. 'Anxious to go in search of the girl? Well you won't have long to wait, the storm's fury is diminishing, in an hour all will be tranquil once more.'

Wolfe nodded, accepting Summers' word as fact, no one knew the deserts as he did.

'I shall come with you,' Summers continued. He held up his hand anticipating Wolfe's protest. 'Don't try to stop me, I'm not an old man yet, you know.'

Coffee entered the room, a tray of refreshments held before her. She was pale, her large eyes soft with tears and, as Summers turned impatiently away from her, Wolfe moved forward to relieve her of her burden.

'Thank you, Coffee,' he said softly. He found himself feeling sorry for the graceful native girl. She had apparently lost favour with her master after giving birth to a still-born son. As yet, Jonathon had not taken another woman to his bed, but it was only a matter of time.

Wolfe sank into a chair, finding it difficult to relax. Garnet's face was always before him; she was so sweet and pale and yet with a flowing mane of bright red-gold hair. She was perhaps the most beautiful thing he'd ever seen. He rose to his feet, impatient with himself. He was becoming soft. So, all right, he was bound to search for her but that didn't mean he should allow himself to be besotted with her.

'There,' Jonathon said in satisfaction. 'See how the wind dies? Now we can prepare to leave for the hills.' A smile crossed his face. 'It will be quite an adventure for me and, you never know, I might even be useful.'

The crying of the baby was loud and insistent, rousing her from the torpor into which she had sunk. She lifted her head and stared before her through eyes that were puffy and swollen, wanting to give up the battle for survival.

The baby struggled against her breasts, his crying fitful now, and Garnet made a supreme effort to rise to her feet. Her legs trembled and her back and arms ached from carrying the child, but she forced herself to stumble forward.

Above her, she heard the flapping of wings and knew with a shudder of horror that she was being followed by grotesque birds of prey. Each step was a nightmare of endurance. The burning sand clung to her legs, dragging her down, and she seemed to be achieving nothing. The desert was slowly but surely beating her into submission.

She flung back her head and screamed out a protest of anger at the sky. She had failed Myrena. She sank down onto her knees, bending her head over Tassili's tiny face. He had fallen silent now, too weak even to cry any more. She lay herself down on the sand, curling into a curve, protecting the baby as much as she could from the heat. In her head was the sound of drums, beating out a steady rhythm. The noise became louder and she lifted herself up, staring across the sand, seeing a flying figure on a black horse coming towards her. In her heat-crazed mind she believed it was death himself. Somehow she rose to her feet, holding Tassili to her breast, screaming that no one would take him from her.

Wolfe's face was above her then and strong arms around her, lifting her from the terrible sand. She still held the baby, her arms refusing to release him, and Wolfe cradled them both. She sighed and closed her eyes, knowing that she would die content.

It was night when Garnet opened her eyes. They felt dry and irritated and it was with difficulty that she looked around and saw she was in a dimly lit room. A candle flickered on a shelf above the doorway and alongside the bed was a table containing a jug of water. She tried to reach out for it but her arm fell back limply to her side.

Had Wolfe been a reality? Hope flowed through her and she closed her eyes against the dry, hot sensation of tears that could not be shed. There was a sound in the doorway and Coffee entered the room, smiling as she saw that Garnet was awake. She poured a cup of water and held it to Garnet's lips, allowing her to drink only a little of the sweet, clear liquid.

Behind her, the concerned face of Jonathon Summers loomed out of the darkness and Garnet knew it was all true. Wolfe had come for her and saved her from the desert.

'Where is he?' she asked Jonathon as he came forward and took her hand in his.

'If you mean my grandson then be assured that he is well and indeed thriving.' He glanced at Coffee. 'She lost her own baby,' he said in a low voice. 'So Kabel's son is a comfort to her and fortunately she has milk enough to feed a dozen little ones.'

Garnet was ashamed that her first thoughts were not for Tassili but for Wolfe. She forced herself to smile at Jonathon, aware that he was proud of the child. It was natural that he should be.

'The boy's mother is dead,' she said slowly. 'But your son Kabel was determined to make his way here, to you, when he had decently buried Myrena.'

Jonathon's face lit up. 'I shall have both my son and a grandson.' His eyes were moist and Garnet's fingers curled in his.

'The baby's name is Tassili,' she said softly. 'It was the name his mother chose. I hope you like it.'

Jonathon nodded his head and turned towards the door. 'I shall leave you to rest now, my dear,' he said. 'In a few days you will be quite recovered, I have no doubt.'

'Jonathon,' Garnet's voice stopped him. 'Wolfe, is he here?' She waited impatiently, her heart beating in sudden fear as she saw the older man shake his head.

'No, he has gone to Tangiers, my dear, business you know, but it was his efforts that saved you.' He shrugged. 'When we made our way towards the foot of the hills, it was some strange instinct that caused Wolfe to veer off to the right. We rode for an hour on what I imagined was a wild goose chase and then we saw you and heard your voice. I could scarcely believe my eyes.'

He smiled at her at the doorway. 'By the time Wolfe returns, your skin will be healed and your beauty will have returned and I'm sure you two will have a great deal to talk about.'

Garnet wanted to ask him what he meant but he lifted his hand in a gesture of farewell and disappeared along the corridor.

For two more days, Garnet was confined to her bed. She had rested there for over a week and her sun-blistered skin was slowly healing with the care lavished upon her by Coffee, who saw Garnet as the benefactress who had given her a beautiful child to care for.

Garnet was at last allowed to dress and join the rest of the household in the dining room for the evening meal. Jonathon fussed around her, placing a cushion behind her, and helped her to the tenderest portions of meat from the platter.

'You look dreadful.' Esther sat opposite Garnet, her eyes glowing with mischief. It was the first time they had seen each other since Garnet's arrival in the house and it was clear that the hostility was still there.

'I know.' Her answer seemed to disconcert Esther who's colour rose.

'I'm sorry,' she said at once, and Garnet smiled. It was foolish to continue the ill-feeling that previously had been a barrier between them.

'Can we be friends?' Garnet said simply. She stared across the table at Esther who was the first to look away.

'I should think you have every reason to be grateful to Garnet, Esther my dear,' Jonathon said mildly. 'She was prepared to die there in the desert rather than abandon the child and continue alone.'

'Please,' Garnet protested at once. 'Don't go believing I was brave or anything like that.'

'But my father is right,' Esther said slowly. 'We all owe you a debt of gratitude. I would like very much for us to be friends.'

Jonathon rose from his chair and stared through the window, his face pensive.

'But Kabel, he should have arrived by now if everything was well with him,' he said. 'I very much fear that he might have perished in the storm.'

Esther went to him, winding her arms around his waist, resting her cheek against his back.

'Do not feel that, Father,' she said. 'There is a hardness present in the Summers family that is not easily extinguished. Kabel will come, I know it.'

Jonathon ruffled her hair, turning to kiss her forehead.

'I pray you may be right, my dear.' He moved away from her. 'But now, forgive me, I will go and see if my grandson is settled for the night.'

Esther returned to the table. 'You are brave, in spite of your protests. I meant what I said, I would be honoured to have you as a friend.'

Garnet smiled. 'Then it is so,' she said softly. She reached out her hand and Esther took it, her face sombre.

'I think Wolfe loves you and there is envy in my heart.' She shrugged. 'But I know I would not fit in with his world and you would do so with grace and beauty. I will content myself with giving my life to caring for my father, remaining with him as is his wish.'

Her words gave Garnet a strange feeling. Could it be possible that Wolfe had fallen in love with her? She felt her heart beating swiftly and she knew in that moment that she loved him with a deep unshakable passion and tenderness. Garnet felt that if he were to declare his love, she would ask for nothing more than to be Wolfe's wife.

It was heartening to see how well Tassili had

adapted to his new mother. When Garnet visited Coffee in her own small room she saw the baby nursed in the native girl's arms, sucking hungrily at her breast. His small hands clutched the golden brown skin around the rosy nipple, his face intent, eyes closed as he dedicated himself to the task of feeding.

Coffee's smile illuminated her face. She spoke softly in her own language and Garnet guessed she was offering her thanks. She sat down beside Coffee, leaning forward to touch Tassili's small cheek. She wondered if, somewhere, Myrena was aware that her child was loved and cared for.

There was a sudden commotion at the front of the building and Garnet rose to her feet, hoping that perhaps Wolfe had returned from Tangiers. She stepped towards the door but fell back as she saw a large figure tower over her.

'Kabel!' She said in amazement. He looked drawn and tired but was not burned and blistered by the sun as she had been. He looked past her to where his baby lay in Coffee's arms and his eyes closed in relief.

'The gods be praised, my son lives.' He entered the room and knelt on the floor and he stared at Coffee as though somehow recognizing her. She smiled slowly at him and reached out her arms, holding the baby towards him.

Kabel took him gently and, as Garnet withdrew from the room, she felt that Kabel would not be long in taking for himself a new wife.

Jonathon was standing in the passageway, his face alight.

'I have my son,' he said. 'He has returned to me. You cannot know how happy I am, Garnet.' He put his arm around her shoulders and together they walked towards the sitting room.

'We shall learn to know each other,' he continued. 'And no more of my children will be sent up into the hills.' He sighed. 'I might as well admit that I grow too old for womanizing. It's about time I settled down. What do you think, my dear?'

Garnet returned his smile, knowing that Jonathon was an old reprobate and, whatever he might say, next week or perhaps the week after there would be a new woman to share his bed.

As they sat opposite each other, Garnet twisted her hands in her lap.

'When do you think Wolfe will come back?' she asked slowly. 'And what sort of business was it that made him leave here so urgently. He couldn't have been fully recovered himself from the days he spent in the desert.'

'Oh, Wolfe is a tough man,' Jonathon said. 'He knows how to survive.'

'You haven't answered my questions,' Garnet said pointedly. Jonathon shrugged.

'You might not like the answer very much.' His eyes met hers in steady regard and Garnet inclined her head.

'Please go on.'

'The woman's name is Lucia Domingo. I believe she and Wolfe were aquainted once.' He rose to his feet and paced the room. 'Her father is offering a great deal of money to have the girl conducted safely to Spain. He provides the ship and crew and apparently insists that Wolfe is the man for the job.' He gave Garnet a quizzical glance. 'That, I believe, is at his spoiled daughter's insistence.'

Garnet felt her heart sink. This then must be the woman from Wolfe's past.

'And what of me?' she asked in a small voice. Jonathon shrugged.

'I believe it may have been Wolfe's intention to take you too, but everything happened too quickly. When we returned with you half-dead from the heat, there was a message waiting for Wolfe. He took off for Tangiers that night.'

So he hadn't even waited to see how she was. Garnet sighed, looking down at her hands.

'Well, thank you for telling me,' she said. 'You have saved me from making myself look very foolish. I should have confessed my love to Wolfe on his return if I hadn't learned about this Lucia Domingo.'

'My dear,' Jonathon's voice was soft. 'We men are strange creatures, you must find it in your heart to make allowances for our weakness.'

'Yes, of course,' Garnet said, but in her heart she knew that Wolfe was anything but weak. He was strong and arrogant and completely selfish. How could she have imagined for one moment that she loved such a man.

'Excuse me, Jonathon.' She rose to her feet. 'I think I shall go to my room and rest. I suddenly feel so very tired.'

CHAPTER THIRTEEN

The waterfront at Tangiers teemed with life. Native bearers scurried along under the hot sun carrying incredible loads on broad, naked shoulders. Sailors of all nationalities walked the weathered boards of the quayside, studying tide and wind with keen interest.

To Wolfe, as he stared from the window of the tavern, the scene was the breath of life. The salt tang of the air was like manna from heaven and he was alive once more to the call of the ocean.

He had been strangely reluctant at first to leave Summers' home with Garnet still exhausted from her ordeal in the heat of the desert. He had experienced the strangest of sensations as he'd seen her stumbling over the sand, the baby clasped to her breasts, her face blistered and burnt. He'd held her in his arms, almost weeping with relief at finding her alive, and the soft weight of her body against his had brought him sweet pleasure.

Then had come the message from Lucia's father. He'd been inclined to refuse the job outright, wanting no more to do with the woman who had given him nothing but bitterness.

He turned as the door behind him opened and Don Domingo entered the room. The tall, distinguished Spaniard had offered him more than he knew. Along with the large sum of money, payment for escorting Lucia to her homeland, he'd given Wolfe the opportunity to return to England with the wherewithal to set himself up in business. On his return to the Summers' residence, it was Wolfe's intention to ask Jonathon to release him from their partnership.

'Ah, it is good to see you, Mr. Surbiton.' Domingo approached him, hand extended, and his clasp was that of an honourable man, firm and strong.

'I believe we can do business together, sir,' Wolfe said affably.

They sat down at the small table and sipped thick dark rum, and Domingo, after scrutinizing Wolfe for a long moment, nodded his head.

'You will accept the assignment?' he asked. Wolfe nodded and was about to speak when the door opened.

'Wolfe! How wonderful to meet with you again.' Lucia was as sweetly beautiful as she had ever been. Her long silky hair was caught up into glossy curls pinned with tortoiseshell combs. Her dark eyes were alight and her scarlet mouth curved upwards.

He rose to his feet, bowing over her white, beringed fingers. She still had the power to send his pulses racing, even though in his mind he knew he was all sorts of a fool.

'Good day to you.' His voice was polite, controlled, and she made a small face at him.

'How formal.' She smiled and sat next to her father,

watching him fill the glasses with the rum from a crystal decanter.

'I am pleased that Mr. Surbiton does not greet you with the easy familiarity displayed by you, Lucia.' His tone was one of disapproval and Lucia kissed his cheek, smiling in amusement.

'Oh, papa, do not be so stuffy.' She leaned back in her chair, her full silk gown of scarlet and green billowing round her slim figure.

'We sail within the week.' Don Domingo spoke as though his daughter had not interrupted. 'I trust that will suit you, Mr. Surbiton?'

Wolfe rose to his feet, sensing that the inverview was at an end.

'One thing,' he said. 'I would wish to bring along a lady. There will be no objections I take it.'

It was Lucia who spoke. 'There is really no room aboard the *Santa Monica* for any other maiden lady but myself,' she said tartly. 'Your job is to protect me from any advances made to me by the officers or crew.' Her eyes stared into his, challengingly, and Wolfe smiled slowly.

'Ah, but by the time we sail, the lady will be my wife,' he said. 'I feel sure your father would approve of a married couple escorting you. It would be much more fitting than a single man as chaperone, don't you agree, Don Domingo?'

The older man rose to his feet. 'The bargain is made. We sail as planned and your wife will be welcomed aboard, sir.'

Wolfe bowed politely and left the tavern. He was

outside then in the heat of the sun with the crush of people pushing past him. He would return to the home of his partner as soon as possible, he decided. There would be a great deal to do before he was ready to sail with the *Santa Monica*.

He looked towards the British brig lying peacefully on the tranquil waters of the bay. There was one task he would have to complete before leaving Tangiers and that was to learn if there was a priest on board. If he was to be married, he would prefer to have an Englishman conduct the service. He approached the quay, looking for a boatsman willing to row him to the brig.

Garnet had bathed herself in the soft waters of the baths, allowing the warm water to lap over her, relieving the tensions of her body and soothing her mind. Today, Wolfe was returning from Tangiers and she had been permanently worried about facing him, afraid he had fallen under the spell of the Spanish girl once more.

She was dressed now in a gown of soft blue that hung over her breasts and clung to the curves of her waist with flattering folds. Her skin was a fresh as a new-born child's now, with no sign of the burns she had received whilst in the desert.

He arrived as she was brushing out her hair. She had heard him enter the house and been aware of Jonathon's loud hearty welcome, but she was unable to move and so remained in the sitting room, breathlessly waiting.

'Garnet,' he said, and she turned to look at him. He was smiling, holding out a parcel towards her.

'I have brought you a few clothes and a new bonnet,' he said, and his eyes seemed to be probing into her very soul.

'Thank you.' She let the brush fall from her hand as he moved nearer, taking her in his arms.

'You look so lovely.' His mouth came down on hers and she clung to him, her eyes closed against the tears of happiness that threatened to spill over onto her cheeks. This was all she wanted, to be held in his arms, to feel his heart beating against her own.

'How do you feel about coming with me to Spain?' He took her face, cupping it in his large hands. 'Then, when my job is done, we could return to England.' He stared down at her and, when she did not answer, he frowned.

'Garnet, don't you understand? I'm asking you to marry me.'

It was as though all her dreams had come true. She lay her face against his shoulder, her hands clinging to him.

'Yes, Wolfe,' she whispered. 'I'll marry you.' He hugged her, lifting her from her feet, spinning her round until she was dizzy. She heard her own laugh and yet tears were salt between her lips. She had never known she could be this happy, ever.

They were married two days later in the fine large room at the front of Jonathon's house. Garnet wore her new gown, the one Wolfe had brought her from Tangiers. It was of soft, white silk with small puffed sleeves and a long satin ribbon tied beneath her breasts. He had not thought to bring her under-clothing, though he had taken the care to purchase a good coat of wool and a fine bonnet with fur edging that sported a bright feather. It was hopelessly old fashioned but she would not have told him so for worlds.

He looked very fine in trousers of nankeen and a silk vest of china blue covered by a single-breasted cut-away coat that emphasized the broadness of his shoulders and the slimness of his waist. She was so proud of him that she could scarcely make her re-sponses to the tired priest's almost casual words. He spoke indistinctly, looking up at the ceiling instead of at the open book resting on his hands. He was hot and weary from his journey which may have accounted for the terse brevity of the ceremony. He closed the book with a snap of finality and Garnet was in Wolfe's arms, happy in the knowledge that she was his wife.

Jonathon had arranged a small celebration for them but, as they were to leave early in the morning to travel with the priest to Tangiers, Wolfe called a halt to the festivities by rising to his feet.

'Please continue to enjoy yourselves, all of you,' he said. 'But I know you will forgive us if we retire early.'

Jonathon smiled, raising his cup high above his head.

'We all wish you health and happiness in your future together,' he said. 'You must know that you will be welcome in my home at any time.'

Garnet looked around her, tears misting her eyes.

She saw Coffee sitting beside Kabel, cradling Tassili in her arms. Behind her was Esther, finger reaching out to touch the baby's tiny hand. It would be difficult to leave them all.

Wolfe's arm was around her shoulder, leading her gently away, and she nestled against him, her cheek against his shoulder, her hand reaching out to touch his fingers as they curled around her waist.

Their bedroom had been hurriedly arranged, but clean bright drapes hung from the bed and the carpet was freshly brushed free of the dust that in this country encroached upon everything.

Wolfe kissed her gently and Garnet closed her eyes, her arms clinging around his neck. She breathed deeply as he touched her breasts beneath the softness of her gown, her nipples stood out firm and hard, responding to his touch.

'Come to bed,' he whispered, his lips kissing her eyelids.

He was gentle, his touch lifting her to the very heights of passion. His hands had not lost their skill and now, mingled with the heat of their desire, was a new tenderness.

He moved within her slowly, intensifying her delight. His mouth was firm against hers and Garnet loved him so much that she longed to cry her happiness out loud.

In the morning, at first light, Garnet was awake. She looked down at Wolfe, sleeping beside her. He was so handsome that she could not resist the impulse to press her lips against his.

He came to her before he was properly roused from sleep. His body was ready and eager for her and she melted into the warmth of his arms.

It was wonderful to belong to him, to know he loved her so much that he had made her his wife. Theirs was no longer a relationship full of doubts, they would be together for always.

He rose from bed at last and stood magnificent in the pale light, staring down at her, his silver-grey eyes half closed. Even now, Garnet realized, she did not know what was going through Wolfe's mind.

'Don't lie there looking so seductive,' he said, smiling. 'Otherwise I might be tempted to come back to bed.'

She leaned up on her elbow, her hair hanging like a curtain across her white breasts.

'Would that be such a bad idea?' She knew she was being deliberately provocative and so did Wolfe. He threw back his head and laughed.

'I'll see you at breakfast,' he said. 'We have to make an early start, remember?'

He left her alone and she sank back against the pillows, savouring her happiness. She could still hardly believe that she was married. She looked at the ring glinting on her finger and a smile curved her lips.

When the time of parting actually came, it was much more difficult than Garnet had anticipated. She held Tassili in her arms for the last time and remembered the journey they had made together through the dust and heat of the desert. She bent and kissed his plump cheek and his dark eyes fluttered open, so like Myrena's that Garnet bit her lip in momentary distress.

'He will be cared for well,' Kabel said gently. 'I will always remember what you do for him and be grateful.'

Coffee took Tassili in her arms and the boy nuzzled her breast searching for food. Garnet smiled and the tension was broken.

'Goodbye, my dear.' Jonathon kissed her cheek. 'I pray you might have a pleasant journey with your proud new husband.'

He shook Wolfe's hand. 'I am sorry to lose you, my partner,' he said regretfully. 'But make a success of your life, my boy, and give this wife of yours a baby of her own to nurse.'

The pony and trap was ready outside the door and Jonathon's servant in scarlet and gold livery was waiting, whip in hand, impatient to be on his way.

Garnet settled herself carefully on the wooden seat, arranging her skirts so that they would not crease. Beside her sat Wolfe and she leaned against him, glad of the solidity of his broad shoulder.

Africa was very beautiful after all, Garnet mused as she turned to wave to the small group standing on the veranda outside the house. Perhaps some day she and Wolfe might return.

She must have turned and waved at least half a dozen times, and Wolfe looked down at her indulgently.

'They are too far away to see you now,' he said. 'Let me see you smile, otherwise I'll begin to believe you are sorry you married me.'

She leaned her head against his shoulder, her hand curling round his fingers.

'I am not sorry,' she said softly. 'It's the best thing that ever happened to me.'

The ground shimmered as the trap bounced along, and in her mind, Garnet was saying her goodbye's all over again. She felt sad when she remembered Myrena's death but she realized she must look forward now to her new life as Wolfe's bride. The past was gone and nothing could change it.

'We're almost there,' Wolfe said. 'See the gleam of the sea in the distance? That, my dear Garnet, is Tangiers.'

CHAPTER FOURTEEN

The small boat bumped gently against the side of the
Santa Monica and Wolfe was on his feet at once, helping
Garnet to negotiate the rope ladder. She laughed as he
lifted her bodily over the rail, his hands lingering on
her waist for a moment before he released her.

'Let me show you to our cabin,' he said teasingly.
'Perhaps we could spend a little time exploring its
comforts before my passenger arrives.'

Garnet's high spirits suddenly vanished. She had
deliberately put all thoughts of Lucia out of her mind.
It had been enough for her that Wolfe had wished to
marry her, assuming that the ghost of his love for the
Spanish girl must be well and truly laid. But now,
faced with the prospect of meeting her in the flesh, she
was a little uncertain of herself.

The ship was luxuriously appointed. Mullioned
windows ranged along the end wall of the cabin and
ornate lanterns hung from the ceiling. Garnet seated
herself in one of the high-backed chairs, arranging her
skirts carefully around her ankles. Wolfe was watching
her, a smile on his lips. He moved to a tin chest

standing beneath one of the windows and flung open the lid.

'You should find some halfway decent clothes in here, Garnet. At least you can pass a few pleasant hours sorting through them. Once we are home, I shall see that you have a completely new wardrobe.'

She saw the array of bright silks and satins and, with a pang of anger, wondered if they were the Spanish girl's cast-offs. She wished Wolfe would come and take her in his arms; he seemed to have become distant and unreachable since they'd entered the cabin. She looked at him from beneath her lashes. He was so handsome in a silk vest over a crisp shirt and plain, dark breeches, she suddenly felt absurdly shy of him.

'When we go to Spain will we visit my Aunt Letticia?' Her voice was formal, not warm as she'd intended. Wolf glanced at her quickly.

'I suppose we must. I had not considered the matter but your family will be anxious for news of you.'

His reluctance angered her. 'Pray do not put yourself to any trouble,' she said tersely.

His silver eyes were suddenly cold. 'I shall not.' He moved to the door. 'Excuse me, there are preparations I have to make.'

Garnet wanted to call him back, to wind her arms around his neck and feel his lips on hers. She could not understand why they were suddenly acting like strangers.

He left her alone and, as the door closed behind him, Garnet rose to her feet, biting her lip, cursing herself for her foolish pride.

She moved round the cabin restlessly. Through the window she could see the sweep of Tangiers bay. The white sand glinted in the sunlight and Garnet felt absurdly homesick, but then Africa had come to mean a great deal to her.

She moved from the window and knelt before the trunk, lifting a silk gown of scarlet edged with black. The folds shimmered before her eyes and a tear fell, darkening the silk.

From above she heard the tinkling sound of a woman's laughter. Growing tense, she hurried to the door and opened it carefully. As she ventured towards the stairs, she could see the straight back of a tall, grey-haired man and, facing him, a strikingly beautiful girl. This then must be Lucia.

The glossy black hair shone with healthy lustre and the flawless skin was creamy, but the most beautiful feature was the girl's eyes. They flashed with vitality under thick dark lashes, staring up now at someone beyond Garnet's line of vision.

She returned to her cabin and leaned against the door. She heard the wind creaking in the timbers and the wash of the pale sea against the ship's side, but she could see the lovely face of the girl Wolfe had loved.

Later, when Wolfe entered the cabin, she could not help but question him.

'Is your passenger safely settled?' There was a note of censure in her voice that he could not fail to notice. His eyes were piercing as he turned towards her.

'Lucia is resting,' he said briefly. Garnet flinched almost visibly at the sound of the girl's name.

'It's charitable of you to take such good care of your passenger,' she found herself saying. 'But then I suppose she means quite a lot to you?'

'Look Garnet,' Wolfe spoke coldly. 'I don't like to be questioned, do I make myself clear?'

She longed to rush into his arms and press her cheek against his and yet she found that she could not do so. Neither could she apologize, so she remained silent.

'Your curiosity will be satisfied,' Wolfe said more amiably. 'We shall all be dining together later.' He picked up a map from the table and it formed an effective barrier between them.

Garnet stared down at her hands clenched together in her lap, telling herself that her fears were unfounded. There was nothing between Lucia and Wolfe. Yet, somehow, the disquieting doubts would not leave her.

She dressed with care that evening, choosing a gown of dark, shimmering green satin, the folds of which fell softly to her feet. The mancherons decorating the shoulders were of black velvet and the same velvet edged the sleeves.

The ship was laid to in harbour until the morning and Wolfe had gone ashore to attend to the details of seeing small quantities of rum and cigars brought on board. He would return any moment and she was determined that when she saw him she would heal the rift that had suddenly opened between them.

She grew anxious when he did not return to the cabin and, at last, she forced herself to go in search of one of the officers.

'Have you seen Mr. Surbiton?' she asked. The sailor stared down at the fullness of her breasts, a strange smile on his swarthy face. He was a Spaniard like the rest of the crew and she was a little intimidated by his fierce eyes and dark moustache.

'He dines with Señorita Lucia, I believe, madam.' He spoke formally enough but there was an edge of derision in his voice that set Garnet's teeth on edge. She spun away from him, anger rising within her. How dare Wolfe do this to her? She felt humiliated and bitterly hurt. But she would not sit alone in the cabin; she would join them for dinner whether they liked it or not.

Lucia's laughter was like a thorn in her flesh as Garnet moved towards the gleaming lights of the forecabin. As she entered, she saw Wolfe bending close to the Spanish girl, pouring a drink into her glass. He glanced up at Garnet, not a bit abashed by her sudden appearance.

'I was just coming to fetch you,' he said, and Garnet forced herself to smile.

'I have saved you the trouble. May I have some wine too?'

She sat down opposite Lucia and saw that the vivacious girl was even more beautiful than she had first thought. Her teeth were white and pearly beneath generous, curving lips as she thanked Wolfe for her drink.

The meal was uncomfortable as Lucia spoke in her perfect English to Wolfe, her eyes sweeping over Garnet to casually include her in the conversation.

She was a woman of superb confidence in herself, convinced of her ability to charm anyone she chose. At this moment, her attention was centred on Wolfe and she wasted no opportunity to touch his arm with her small, slender fingers.

Garnet found herself sinking into a deep silence. She had no intention of competing with Lucia for Wolfe's smiles. Let him be captivated by the Spanish girl's facile charm if he was so gullible.

Wolfe rose to his feet at last, throwing down his napkin. He bowed formally.

'Excuse me, ladies. There is still a great deal that needs my attention below decks. Perhaps you two would like to become better acquainted without the encumbrance of a mere man to put a curb on your gossip.'

When he had gone, Lucia leaned across the table, staring wide-eyed at Garnet.

'Are you jealous of me?' she said bluntly, and Garnet was surprised at the brazenness of her question. Without waiting for a reply, Lucia continued.

'You should be. Wolfe and I are so close, as you can see.'

Garnet leaned back in her chair, determined to keep tight rein on her temper.

'Not so close,' she said softly. 'Otherwise why did he marry me and not you?'

Lucia smiled. 'I can answer that.' She placed her fingertips together, her eyes cold. 'My father would allow only a married man to escort me to Spain. Wolfe took you as his wife in order to be nearer me.' She laughed deprecatingly. 'My papa believe me an innocent, poor dear, he thought my honour would be safe with the presence of another woman on board.'

Garnet felt her control slipping. 'But what good can it do you to be close to him?' she asked carefully. 'You know nothing can come of the relationship.'

Lucia rose and flounced her skirts around her slim ankles. Her eyes flashed towards Garnet.

'Really, you are naïve as papa!' She shook back her glossy hair. 'It is not marriage I want of Wolfe, nor he of me, it is something far more basic than that.'

'I shall see what Wolfe has to say about all this.' Garnet rose to her feet, her face flushed with anger. 'I don't believe that he would have an affair with you under my very nose.'

'No?' Lucia was unflustered. 'Then why was he alone with me in this very cabin for most of the afternoon?' She smiled again. 'Run along, ask your husband questions, it will do you no good.'

Garnet's heart was beating fast as she made her way towards her own cabin. Wolfe was standing within the doorway and he waited for her to enter.

'What is there between this woman and you?' she asked at once. 'Are you continuing the affair you started with her years ago?'

'Calm down, Garnet.' Wolfe's voice was dangerously quiet. He closed the door before turning to her. She did not wait for him to speak again.

'Do you deny that you find her attractive?' she demanded, and she saw his eyes narrow.

'No, I deny nothing,' he said shortly. She could see that he was angry but she could not stop the rush of questions.

'Did you marry me simply to take this trip, so that it would be possible for you to escort Lucia to Spain?'

He shook his head. 'If I said no, it would be a lie.' He stared at her and she could not read his expression. 'But I do not intent to explain my actions to you. As my wife, I expect a little trust from you.'

'Trust! You don't know the meaning of the word.' She stared at him defiantly. 'I wish to be taken ashore. I will not remain with you a moment longer, not to be used as a cover for your affairs with this Spanish woman.'

'Very well,' Wolfe said shortly. 'Pack your belongings. I will arrange for the boat to be ready in fifteen minutes.'

He turned and left her and Garnet stared at the closed door in stricken silence. He had not even made a pretence of caring for her. He was allowing her to go, no, more, he was making it possible for her to leave him. She sank down into a chair and covered her face with her hands.

'Wolfe!' She spoke his name with a sense of anguish. If he had only given her one small sign that he cared she would have thrown herself into his arms. She would have persuaded him that he would be happy with her, that she was his wife for all time. But he had coldly agreed to her leaving the ship. She was no longer needed. The Spanish man had gone, leaving his daughter on board the *Santa Monica*. The lovers could be together now without constraint.

She could not believe that Wolfe would not relent even as she went up on deck with a small bag over her arm. He was nowhere to be seen but one of the sailors moved forward to help Garnet into the unsteady boat bobbing at the ship's side.

Garnet watched the oars dipping into the silvered waters and her eyes were blurred with tears she was too proud to shed. Her brief marriage was over before it had really begun and she was going out of Wolfe's life for ever.

From the cabin window, watching the small boat disappearing over the sea towards the harbour of Tangiers, Wolfe was wondering if he had been too hasty. But Garnet's high-handedness had angered him and he had been determined to teach her a lesson. She had forced him into a corner, putting her own interpretations on his motives for marrying her, and that he would not tolerate.

Well, she could just cool her heels for a little while. He had paid the Spanish officer well to take Garnet to Jonathon Summers' home for a few weeks; she could wait there until his task of delivering Lucia safely to Spain was accomplished. He would return to fetch her and take her to England and perhaps she would be less eager to rail at him when she'd had a little time to think.

He turned as he heard a knock on the door and, without waiting for his bidding, Lucia entered the cabin, smiling at him seductively.

'I see you sent the English girl away,' she said, her tongue moistening her lips. She came close to him, her white hand resting on his shoulder. 'Did you quarrel over me, Wolfe?'

He felt exasperated. He was a man unused to women complicating his life. He stared down at Lucia and he felt the last traces of his infatuation for her vanish. He could see her as she really was, a beautiful but rather shallow woman. He could scarcely envisage her battling through the desert to save the life of another woman's child.

'Lucia,' he said quietly. 'Would you please return to your own cabin?'

She pouted up at him. 'Don't be angry with me, Wolfe, you know how charming I find you.'

'It's over, Lucia,' he said deliberately. 'I am being paid to take you home and that is the extent of my interest in you, do you understand!'

She drew away from him and stared upwards, reading the truth in his eyes.

'You fool,' she said. 'You are in love with your wife, how very sweet, and its all too boring for words.'

'Your derision changes nothing,' he said, suddenly at ease. 'You are right, I love my wife.' He bundled Lucia from the cabin and closed the door on her furious face. He smiled as he poured himself a drink from the decanter on the table. She was right about him being a fool, too; by his pigheadedness, he had deprived himself of Garnet's company for what might be as much as two long weeks. He lifted the glass of sparkling wine high and looked into the crystal depths, making a silent vow. Once he was reunited with Garnet, he would see they were never parted again.

CHAPTER FIFTEEN

As the *Santa Monica* grew smaller on the horizon, Garnet began to feel frightened. She had been precipitate in leaving the ship so thoughtlessly; now she was beginning to wonder what she would do next.

The Spanish officer sitting opposite her, rowing the boat in silent concentration, had given her no indication that he'd received any orders from Wolfe. It appeared she was being summarily abandoned on the sands of Tangiers to fend for herself. Anger grew within her, giving her courage.

'Wait,' she said. 'See the British brig over there, I wish you to put me on board instead of taking me to the shore.'

The man stared at her, frowning a little. It appeared he had difficulty with his English because he looked in the direction where she was pointing and shook his head.

'Yes. I insist,' she said, almost pleadingly. He stared at her for a moment and then shrugged. It seemed he wanted no responsibility for her. He dipped the oar into the water, turning the small craft, and within a

surprisingly short time, they were alongside the brig.
The ship was low in the water, no doubt heavily laden
with fresh supplies of food and water. She had no idea
what she would say when she met the captain, but,
dimly, she hoped she could persuade him to take her
home to England.

He was a burly man with a genial smile, splendid in
a black topcoat lined with scarlet and bearing a row of
silver buttons.

'Captain Maynard at your service, madam.' He
held out a chair in his cabin for her to sit down and he
rubbed his hands together staring at her with barely
concealed curiosity.

'Welcome to my humble ship, dear lady. It is far
from palatial but it serves the purpose, yes indeed it
does.' He seated himself on the opposite side of the
table and looked at her in silence, waiting for her to
make her position clear.

'I need your help, Captain Maynard,' she said in a
rush. 'I wish to return to my father's home in
England.'

'Well that does not seem to present any difficulties.'
The captain smiled and Garnet was aware that he was
not as amiable as she had first thought him. His eyes
were a little too close set and his mouth was a thin line.

'Well, there is a problem' she said nervously. 'I have
no money, you see.'

'Ah!' The word came out on a sigh. The captain
pushed himself to his feet with an effort. 'That's too
bad, too bad indeed.'

'But my father is a fairly wealthy man,' Garnet said

quickly. 'If you would trust me for the passage money until we return home you would be well compensated for your trouble.'

'I see.' The captain rubbed his plump hands together. 'So the position is this. You wish to travel in my ship, eat my food and drink my wine without even a piece of jewellery or gold, perhaps, as surety, is that it?'

Garnet felt her colour rise. 'I have nothing,' she said. She rose to her feet. 'But I shouldn't have troubled you with my problems.'

He held up his hand. 'Now there is no need for haste. Please allow me to think about this, madam.' He placed his cap on his balding head. 'If you will forgive me, there is something that needs my attention. Please remain in my cabin and rest. I shall have refreshments brought to you.'

At the door he turned to look at her and his gaze made Garnet strangely uneasy.

'Have you no friends, no relatives in Africa who could help you?' he asked.

Garnet shook her head, unable to answer. She had never felt so alone and humiliated in all her life. The captain thrust his hands into his pockets, straining the material of his trousers at the seams.

'Excuse me,' he said, and closed the door behind him, leaving Garnet scarlet-faced and uncomfortable. She closed her eyes and leaned back in her chair. Whatever the circumstances aboard the *Santa Monica* they would have at least been more bearable than laying herself at the mercy of a man like Captain Maynard whose chief concern seemed to be in lining his own pockets.

She walked around the small airless cabin restlessly. She wondered what Wolfe was doing at this very moment. She closed her eyes as she imagined him holding Lucia in his arms, kissing her tenderly, possibly declaring his love for her. She felt suffocated, perhaps a turn around the deck would freshen her thoughts, clear her mind of useless regrets. She went to the door and, as she tried to open it, she became aware that it was securely locked. Her mouth was dry as she stared around her in panic. Why would the captain who seemed reluctant to even have her on board make her a prisoner?

She tugged harder on the door, calling out for help, but it seemed that no one heard her. At last she sank down into a chair once more and rested her head wearily on the polished surface of the table. She longed for the relief of tears but they would not come.

There was the scratch of a key turned in the lock and into the cabin came a sailor carrying a tray. He was not an officer. He was dressed in a stained shirt with a coarse cloth around his neck and, when she spoke to him, she realized with a sinking of her heart that he was not even English.

'The captain,' she said, slowly. 'Where is he?' She drew nearer to the man, hoping to dodge past him, but he moved backwards, his bulk filling the doorway. He shook his head as she repeated the question and retreated quickly, slamming the cabin door with a resounding bang.

Garnet stared down at the tray. It contained a plate

of greasy mutton and a cup of rum and she turned
away from it in disgust.

It was over an hour later when she heard the door
being unlocked once more. This time it was the captain himself who stood smiling down at her. Garnet
rose in a fury and faced the man squarely.

'How dare you keep me locked up?' she said fiercely.
'I won't be treated this way. I demand you release me at
once. I would rather stay on shore than sail with you.'

'Silence,' Captain Maynard said. His smile was
gone and there was a greedy light in his eyes.

'Now, sit down, have a little patience and I shall tell
you what your future is to be.'

Garnet sank into a chair, staring up at the man, her
heart beating swiftly.

'What do you mean?' she asked, and he smiled. He
did not reply at once. He walked around her, deliberately taking in every detail of her appearance.

'Well, who would have thought it,' he said, rubbing
his plump hands together. 'You have been having
some wonderful adventures whilst in Africa I believe,
dear lady.'

'What I have done is none of your business,' Garnet
said uneasily. 'Just let me go, that's all I want of you.'

'Come now,' he said smiling faintly. 'Don't be un-
friendly. Tell me about your stay with the hill women.
Is it true they have only one man between them all?'

Garnet sat in silent dread, looking into the man's
beady eyes that regarded her now with speculation.
There was a reason other than base curiosity behind
his questions.

He was watching her steadfastly, waiting with ill-concealed impatience for her to answer him. She pressed her lips together, determined to remain quiet. If she told him anything at all about her time spent in Africa it would surely encourage further questions.

He put his head on one side. 'No matter.' He shrugged. 'But I will tell you my thoughts. If I go to the expense of removing you to England, it could well be that your father would not wish to have such a daughter returned. You do see what I mean dear lady?'

She closed her eyes, not wanting to look at the vile man or even to listen to his voice. What did it matter if he thought her the lowest strumpet in Tangiers? The worst he could do would be to dump her back on land and leave her there. All the same, it pained her to realize that the man thought her fallen, without pride or virtue. He held her in such low esteem that he could speak to her so insultingly, without redress.

There was a sharp knocking on the door that startled Garnet. She sat up straight in her chair as the captain slowly moved round the table. A man entered the cabin dressed in a hooded robe from beneath which jutted a hooked nose and a cruel mouth.

He stood looking down at Garnet for a moment and then caught her chin in his hard fingers, twisting her head to one side.

'My dear Sulimary Ali, is the girl not all I described to you?' Captain Maynard spoke ingratiatingly, his hands moving together as though he was washing them.

'She appears well favoured, though a trifle skinny

for my taste.' The man drew Garnet to her feet and held her wrist in a cruel grasp. 'Her hair is like fire but what is beneath these thick clothes? Is the girl marked, or ugly?'

'Look for yourself, my dear Ali.' Captain Maynard folded his fat hand over his stomach and stood back, his eyes alight with curiosity.

'Leave me alone.' Garnet's voice was low with anger. 'I have no intention of allowing you to treat me as a slave.'

It was as though the man had not heard her speak. He pushed her across the table, casually lifting her skirts. His hands were running over her breasts and across the slender curve of her hips.

'That is enough to tell me she is not spoiled by child-bearing,' he said, releasing her abruptly. Garnet gasped, unable to believe what was happening.

'Then you are satisfied that the girl will make a good bondservant?' The captain smiled. 'Good, yes indeed, that is very good. Now we can get down to business.'

Garnet, seeing the two men were preoccupied, made a sudden rush for the door. She jerked it open and ran into the passageway and was halfway up the stairs when her hair was caught and her head jerked backwards, dragging her to the floor.

'I see you must be taught obedience.' Sulimary Ali was unsmiling. His dark-skinned face set in lines of displeasure. He pulled her back into the cabin and slapped her face hard. She reeled away from him, falling helplessly to the floor.

'The price, my dear Ali. What is it you are offering

for this spirited flower of English womanhood?' The captain mopped his face with a silk kerchief and sat down, signalling for his guest to take a seat opposite him. He lifted a crystal decanter from the shelf and poured a large measure of rum for each of them.

Sulimary Ali stared at Garnet as she lay on the rough boards of the cabin. His dark eyes assessed her possible value, he put his hand inside his robe withdrawing a cloth of velvet.

'She is not worth much,' he said. 'She is a bond-servant, not a wife.'

The captain smiled and continued to pour rum into the man's glass. He shrugged and waited silently for Sulimary Ali to make him an offer.

'There will be a great deal of prestige for you, my dear Ali,' he said after a long silence. 'A beautiful white girl is not found on every street corner.'

Ali drank a little from the cup, his dark eyes watching as Garnet rose unsteadily to her feet and sat on the bunk, trying to regain the breath that had been knocked from her body by her fall. He placed the cloth on the table and leaned back.

Captain Maynard deftly folded back the corners of the velvet, smiling as he saw a shining gold ornament resting in the folds. The brooch was in the shape of a salamander with two burning rubies for eyes.

'Ah, yes, very nice.' The captain scooped the brooch up in one quick movement and placed it in his waist-coat pocket. He rose to his feet and bowed with almost comical dignity. 'I trust we are both satisfied, dear Ali.'

Without a word, the man rose from his chair and caught Garnet around her throat, drawing her towards the door. She tried to struggle free but it was impossible to breathe so she fell still, helpless against Ali's cruelty.

Four men waited on deck and, at a few quietly spoken words from Sulimary Ali, took hold of Garnet's arms, lifting her bodily off her feet, covering her in a smothering blanket.

She felt herself being placed face down in a boat and the damp of the boards seeped through the coverings around her. She could feel the swell of the ocean and realized the craft was heading into open waters.

She tried to move and ease the intolerable ache in her shoulders but a sharp kick against her back forced her to remain still. Her head was in a whirl, she still felt that she was in a nightmare from which she must surely awake. Only a short while ago she had left the shores of Africa as a happily married woman and now she had been abducted by an evil-looking stranger whose intention it was to make her a servant in his house.

The stifling fold of the blanket fell away from her face and gratefully she breathed the cold night air. Above her head, the moon was a silver orb and to the west lay high, jagged cliffs, the tops silvered as though covered in snow.

At last, the boat bumped against the sands of a small, quiet cove that boasted nothing more than the crudest of jetties. Garnet was flung across the shoulder of one of the men and she heard his curses as his feet slipped against the stones of the beach.

They were climbing up the rocky face, along a narrow pathway, and Garnet began to shiver in the cold of the night air. Her head hung downwards, her long hair swinging from side to side and she felt as though the breath was forced from her body as the man pressed on upwards, carrying her as though she were a bale of cloth.

She had given up hope of escaping from Sulimary Ali. It was as if all her spirit had been drained from her. She was set on her feet, falling at once to her knees in the harsh soil, not caring if she was left there to die.

Before her, against the silver of the sky, she saw domed minarets pointing upwards in dark relief. She closed her eyes, too weary to think or feel or even to protest when one of the men jerked her to her feet, pushing her forward with sharp words she could not understand.

Her body obeyed from instinct, her legs moving though devoid of sensation. She was beneath a great arch now, with fierce guards standing to attention on either side of a curved door. Another push sent her through into a large tiled courtyard with twin fountains lit by glowing lanterns.

She heard Sulimary's voice speaking harshly and she was led along a richly carpeted corridor under the brilliant light from large chandeliers of copper and wood hanging from richly painted ceilings.

The passageways became darker, with bare stone floors and only dim lanterns to penetrate the gloom. A huge woman appeared from behind a great heavy door and nodded as the man thrust Garnet forward.

She was inside a separate part of the great building then, where there were only women. She heard the dull thud as the door was bolted behind her and her heart sank as she realized she was now a part of Sulimary Ali's seraglio.

CHAPTER SIXTEEN

Garnet found she was not privileged as were the other women in the seraglio. They were entitled to spend the days beautifying themselves in readiness for the attentions of their lord and master.

The older women spent long hours dying greying hair with henna or painting dark lines around their eyes, trying desperately to appear more youthful.

Garnet as a bondservant was expected to pander to the favoured ones, bringing them sugared water or cervosa, a herbal drink served ice cold in tall goblets. She had attempted to protest at first but found very quickly that rebellion in a seraglio was swiftly punished.

Marhabba was the kadin, a grotesquely fat woman who had borne five strong sons to Sulimary Ali. Her position was unshakable and she ruled the women with severity, lashing them with her tongue, and, when that failed, enforcing her orders with a small whip of hairs that stung when applied vigorously against bare flesh.

She took an immediate dislike to Garnet and was

prepared to show her disfavour at the slightest provocation. She gave the white woman the most menial of jobs and Garnet spent hours crouched over the fire in the kitchen baking bud, a form of bread cooked beneath the heat of the coals.

Sometimes the servants were given, as a treat, coarse hog meat that ran with fat. Garnet preferred to eat only boiled rice spiced with raisins in spite of Marhabba's venomous looks when she turned away the platter of meat. The kadin longed for everyone to be as fat as she. Her very flesh trembled when she walked and she had lost favour with her lord in latter years. Anyone considered to be a rival was sorely treated, tasting the sting of the whip frequently. Garnet was unfortunate enough to have attracted the attention of the ladies by her long red hair and white skin and therefore had been marked down as an enemy by the kadin at once.

Since she had arrived at the seraglio a week ago, Garnet had seen nothing of Sulimary Ali. As the days passed and she was left alone to work in the kitchens, she began to feel that the danger was past. She was continually covered in dust and grease and her hair was twisted into a severe knot on her head, so that she felt no man, let alone a sultan who owned hundreds of women, would find her attractive. She had noticed that when a woman was summoned to the master, she was bathed and her clothes changed from head to toe. A woman never appeared before her lord twice in the same costume.

As Garnet became used to her surroundings, she

began to form a plan of escape. To one side of the enormous complex of buildings was the cliffs and the sea. Without a boat she had no hope of fleeing in that direction. She would have to explore the ground to the front of the seraglio; perhaps she would find a road or at least a pathway leading back to Tangiers.

The difficulty was to evade Marhabba's eagle eye. The woman took great satisfaction in putting upon Garnet every menial task she could find. There was scarcely any time for Garnet to be alone; she was busy in the kitchen until the bell rang for devotions. By then she was so tired that it was a relief to fall onto her pallet and sleep.

Her moment came at last when Marhabba was summoned to her lord. There was great excitement in the seraglio; it was a long time since the kadin had been so honoured. Garnet surpressed her eagerness, helping with apparent docility to dress the gross woman in her best attire, knowing that once the kadin had left the seraglio, she would be left to her own devices.

The drawers of thin, rose-coloured damask were drawn over Marhabba's huge legs. She struggled into the brocaded pantaloons with difficulty, having put on a great deal of flesh since last she had worn them. She used her whip frequently, her face red with beads of moisture covering her wide forehead.

A smock of fine white silk gauze was closed at the neck with a diamond, the wide sleeves straining over the kadin's upper arms. Through the soft material, the woman's enormous breasts could be clearly seen. She smiled her delight, making lewd gestures to show that her lord would admire her fullness.

The waistcoat of white and gold damask was intended to fit closely at the waist, but instead, it jutted out like two wings, the fringes of gold silk flapping around the great bulge at Marhabba's stomach.

She sank down cautiously on a stool, puffing with the exertion. She called Garnet with loud harsh tones and showed by gestures that she needed some sugar water to revive her. When the white woman did not at once understand, she aimed a vicious blow with her whip and laughed as the girl moved away quickly.

Shoes of leather kid, embroidered with gold, were forced onto the kadin's bulging feet. Her eyes stood out from her head and it seemed she would be unable to rise and stand, let alone make her way down the network of corridors to the suite of rooms occupied by Sulimary Ali.

She fanned herself with her hand, laughing like a young girl, enjoying the attention and looks of envy she was receiving from the other wives.

With much heaving and a great deal of talk, the kadin was at last upright and a wide band of satin encrusted with diamonds was placed around her middle. A curdee, a cloak of satin lined with ermine, was placed upon Marhabba's shoulders and, at last, she was ready.

The retinue of wives went with her towards the huge door that was the dividing line between the seraglio and the rest of the buildings. Garnet was in the midst of the crowd of eager, gossiping women and, when a eunuch opened the bolts, she slipped through into the dimness of the corridor beyond. With a quick look around, she concealed herself in an alcove and watched as the women retreated back into the seraglio, leaving Marhabba to walk the rest of the way accompanied only by the eunuch.

Breathlessly, Garnet waited until the lumbering figure of the kadin was out of sight. She cautiously peered from her hiding place then and tried to gauge where she was.

There was no point in heading in the direction of the front door; it was guarded too closely. She could only hope there was another way out of the widely spread buildings.

The sound of footsteps ringing against the bare flagstones startled Garnet. She slipped behind a curtain and held her breath in fear. She heard voices and closed her eyes in dread as the footsteps halted a short distance from where she was hidden. The voices were deep, speaking in the harsh tongue that was so foreign to her ears. She heard the name of Sulimary Ali and then, to her relief, the men began to move away, their voices dying in the distance.

She sped along the cold stone passageway behind them, careful to keep her distance. They paused once more, deep in conversation, and she was forced to crouch in the shadows, praying they would continue on their way before someone else came along the corridor and saw her.

It seemed that fate was with her. The two men at last passed through a door, hidden behind a hanging carpet and, after a moment, Garnet followed them. The yard in which she found herself was an open square, brilliant with sunshine, and at the far end was a gate. There was nowhere to hide. She would just have to run as fast as she could and hope she would not be seen.

She tensed herself, ready for the ordeal, and with a last, desperate glance at the windows of the building overlooking the yard, she was speeding across the dusty ground. She reached the gate and all around her there was a dreaming sunlit silence. She took a deep breath, the alarm had not been given, she had not been seen.

Through the gate was a narrow pathway overhung with trees. The shade was cool and green and Garnet looked around her in wonder, tasting freedom and yet still fearing discovery.

The small track seemed endless and, just as she was despairing of ever finding the end of it, she saw another gate, heavy and metallic, emblazoned with eagles of bronze that flashed in the sunshine.

Cautiously, she went forward and realized that she was behind the seraglio with the high wall facing her and the gateway her only means of escape. With a sense of excitement mingled with fear, she crept forward, towards the small wooden hut where she imagined a guard would be posted. The heat was intense, and even before she reached the doorway of the shelter, she heard deep snoring coming from within. The capigis was asleep.

The gate was unlocked. Garnet opened a gap just

wide enough for her to slip through and then she was running, as though she would never stop, across the sparse grasslands that bordered the building. Her heart was beating so swiftly, she could hardly breathe and her eyes were misted with beads of perspiration as the sun beat down on her bare head.

Ahead of her was a dusty plain and Garnet could see no roadway or any sign of habitation. She paused for a moment, trying to calm her fears, straining her eyes to see into the distance. Rolling flatlands stretched out before her, offering nothing but sand and heat. She swerved, changing direction, and a cooler breeze coming off the sea brought the tang of salt to her nostrils.

She found herself on the clifftop, looking down at the placid waters of the bay. Her foot slipped a little on the loose stones and she clutched at a bush to steady herself. It was then she heard the sound of loud voices, calling excitedly behind her.

Without thought for her safety, she ran down the steep track and along the clinging sand towards the ocean. She did not think coherently about how she would survive in the vast expanse of water that stretched as far as she could see. She plunged into the blue-green depths and struck out, swimming with frantic strength, aware that on the beach behind her stood the guards, calling instructions to each other.

Her strength was waning, she felt herself sink beneath the surface of the sun-bright sea. She was slipping into a state of semi-consciousness where nothing seemed to matter. Strong hands caught and held her and, though she struggled, she was carried up onto the hot sand where she lay, gasping for breath.

Later, when she had been returned to the seraglio and placed in a locked room, Marhabba came to her. She was enraged by Garnet's attempt to escape the moment her back was turned and lashed at her with the horse-hair whip, talking furiously, her over-large eyes protruding from her red face.

Her meeting with the sultan had left her in no better frame of mind. On the contrary, she was in a worse temper than ever Garnet had seen her.

Garnet was still wearing the small pantaloons and waistcoat that was the garb of the bondservant. The clothes were wet from the sea and clung to her slender body concealing nothing. With a look of disgust, Marhabba went to the door and called loudly, bringing a flurry of women to her side.

One of the eunuchs stood behind the women and it was he who explained to Garnet what was happening.

'The master will speak with you,' he said. 'You must be washed and prepared to enter his magnificent presence.' He backed away when Marhabba cursed him roundly, flaying his black skin with her whip, berating him until he fell back from the doorway, his round eyes rolling in fear of the kadin.

Garnet was at last taken from the small room and led into a part of the seraglio she had never seen before. The large chamber was tiled in exquisite colours and at the far end was a bath sunken deep into the floor.

Marhabba pushed her forward impatiently, pulling at her clothing and gesturing towards the scented water. Garnet could do nothing else but obey, though her spirits were low and she dreaded the coming meeting with Sulimary Ali.

As she washed herself in the sweet-smelling water, she suddenly thought of Wolfe. She had deliberately forced any memories of him from her mind, but now they came flooding back and she felt tears burn her eyes.

She had lain in his arms, known the joy of becoming his wife, and then she had found that he had deceived her. Theirs had been a marriage of convenience, little more than a cloak to cover his affair with Don Domingo's beautiful daughter. But worse even than the knowledge that he wanted this other woman was the realization that he had allowed her to leave the ship, to take her future in her own hands without even trying to follow her and make sure she was safe. She simply had to accept the fact that he did not care what became of her.

Marhabba was calling to her, gesturing wildly with her plump hands, and Garnet sighed, climbing up the steps of the bath with a feeling of hopelessness drifting over her. She stood passively as the kadin gave orders for her to be dressed properly to meet the sultan.

Her garments were not as magnificent as the ones that Marhabba had worn, but then Garnet was only a bondservant. Nonetheless, she was clothed in silk pantaloons embroidered with gold and silver flowers and a waistcoat of heavy satin was placed over a blouse of soft silk. She was given plain sandals for her feet and the kadin stood back, pointing a finger at

Garnet's breasts, laughing as she compared them to her own heavy fullness. She gave her a push that almost sent Garnet spinning to the floor and her momentary humour disappeared.

Garnet's long hair was combed and a small silk cap sewn with seed pearls was placed on her head. Over this, Marhabba hung a veil and, then, it seemed, she was satisfied.

The eunuch was given the task of accompanying Garnet to Sulimary Ali's rooms. He looked down with wide brown eyes and, once they were outside the heavy door, he allowed himself a sigh of relief.

'She hate you,' he said. 'She expect master to take her to his bed but he only ask her to prepare you, she mad with jealousy, she do you harm if she can.'

Garnet's immediate concern was the sultan, not Marhabba. The kadin could inflict the miseries of working in the kitchen and flaying her with her whip but the sultan could do so much more. He might even feel he would like to take her to his bed and she shuddered at the thought.

'You be good to master, he see you treated well,' the eunuch said gently. 'He stop the kadin beating you and making you work like slave. He keep you nice, give you easy life if you his woman.'

He meant well but Garnet knew she could not bear Sulimary Ali's touch. She remembered with horror how he had run his hands over her body before buying her from Captain Maynard, his fingers insensitive, his face a mask of cruelty. How could she even pretend to accept his attentions?

The eunuch led her into a richly carpeted room at the centre of which was a vast, circular bed hung with long, diaphanous drapes. The curtains at the arched window were of rich velvet encrusted with precious stones. On a low table stood a silver jug surrounded by tall goblets of crystal with silver handles.

'Remember,' the eunuch said softly. 'Please the master and you will be well rewarded.'

Garnet was left alone then and she stood at the centre of the room, surrounded by opulence, her head bent beneath the heavy veil, her eyes wide with fear as she waited for Sulimary Ali to come to her.

CHAPTER SEVENTEEN

'Well, Lucia, this is where we say goodbye.' Wolfe held her hand briefly as she stood at the rail of the *Santa Monica*, the coast of Spain shimmering in the heat behind her.

'You won't change your mind and come ashore even for a few days?' Lucia asked, her dark eyes flashing as she stared up at him, her red lips parted into a smile.

'No, I won't change my mind.' Wolfe turned and went below to his cabin with a sigh of relief. It was good to have accomplished his mission, especially after the difficulties he had run into on the voyage. The ship had sprung a leak and was hove to off Tangiers for several days before he could even set off, and during that time he had fumed with impatience, cursing himself for a fool for sending Garnet away. He could only hope that she was not too unhappy with Jonathon Summers. At least she would have Coffee and Tassili to occupy her time and Esther, with whom she could exchange confidences if she so wished. He smiled, imagining her reporting indignantly about his arrogance in sending her back to the Summers' residence. If only she knew how much he had regretted his actions.

The *Santa Monica* had run into a freak storm a few miles out from Spain and he had been delayed still further, but now, with Lucia safely bound for shore, he could put all his energies into the return journey.

It was strange, he mused, that his meeting with Lucia had turned out so differently from what he had expected. She had haunted him for so long, the sting of his rejection by her cutting deep, and yet she had been the means of revealing how important Garnet really was to him.

He poured a good measure of rum and sat in his chair, his boots resting on the footstool before him. He smiled, picturing Garnet's face when he arrived to take her home. He had no doubt that she would be furious at first. Her small, pale face would be like a folded rose-petal as she frowned at him. Her tangled, vivid hair would be spread around her shoulders like a silk cape. He would take her in his arms and kiss away her anger and confess to her that he had suffered many sleepless nights without her beside him.

He could hardly believe now that he had been so long in finding out that he loved Garnet. But then he had allowed the hurt inflicted by Lucia to cloud his mind and his judgement. He wondered what sort of man her father would be. That he cared about his daughter very much indeed was evident. Hadn't he sent her away from England and the state of unrest that had almost cost him his life? By now, he must be giving up hope of ever seeing his child again.

Wolfe rose to his feet, there was no point sitting around brooding. Far better if he got out his maps and did some work. Soon, with the turn of the tide, the *Santa Monica* would take up her anchor and set out on the return journey to Tangiers.

Perhaps when they reached the harbour, he would stop just long enough to buy Garnet the new gowns he had promised her. For too long she had made do with other women's cast-offs. His blood raced as he thought of her smooth white body. She was so small, so perfect, and yet with such inner strength.

He threw down the unopened chart and went up on deck once more, staring across the bay, wondering if he should go ashore after all. It was making him restless just sitting around waiting for the next tide. Perhaps a drink in one of the taverns with some cheerful company would ease the ache within him.

Castellon was a tiny port on the south coast of Spain. As he stepped onto the shore from the small rowing boat, Wolfe looked round him curiously. A fisherman sat mending his nets, a pipe jutting from thin lips. His dark eyes watched as Wolfe tied up the boat and walked through the yellow sand. On the one cobbled street was an array of shops and taverns, and it was to the largest of these that Wolfe made his way.

He did not see the fisherman nod to a small urchin swinging bare feet into the foam at the edge of the water. If he had, he would doubtless have given the matter a second thought.

He was seated in the window, drinking a mug of ale,

when the three men came towards him. There was a menace in the way they walked, striding forward with purpose. He rose to his feet, his back against the wall, and it was then he recognized the officer to whom he had entrusted Garnet's safe keeping. The man had not returned to the ship but Wolfe had assumed he had missed the tide and would be waiting when the *Santa Monica* returned to Tangiers.

He stared at the man, waiting for him to say something that would enlighten him as to the purpose of his appearance.

'You have come for me, Mr. Surbiton?' The officer stared at him with dark, unreadable eyes. 'You want your money back, no?'

He smiled and it was clear he had been drinking heavily. Wolfe tried to think clearly. Why should Officer Zaragosa imagine he would want his money back unless he had not completed his task properly? He suddenly felt cold.

'The money is not important,' he spoke slowly, aware that the man's English was not good. 'But the lady, my wife, where is she?'

Zaragosa threw his hands wide, speaking swiftly in Spanish. He stepped away from Wolfe and then suddenly swung his fist in a wild gesture designed to knock the Englishman to the ground.

He missed completely, but then his companions were surging forward, eager to fight the man who undoubtedly carried with him a fat purse.

Wolfe stepped aside, catching the larger of the men a punishing blow on the back of his neck. He went down like a felled tree and lay still. The other man, with a frightened look at Wolfe, sped away.

'That leaves just you and me, Zaragosa,' Wolfe said in a low, angry voice. 'Tell me where the lady is or I'll cut your ears off.'

'She went to English ship.' The man was subdued now that he faced Wolfe alone. 'Captain Maynard, he know what happen to her. He bring me here to Spain two days ahead of the *Santa Monica*. We pass you when you have repairs done.' He paused and spread his hands wide. 'But lady not on board. I not see her.'

Wolfe shook the man and for a moment he was blinded by rage. He dropped Zaragosa to the ground and stepped over his cowering body, realizing he was wasting time.

It was hot outside in the street and he put his hands to his forehead, staring out to where the English brig was anchored to the port of his own ship. He wondered why the captain had brought her so far easterly; it was not the normal route for shipping. He himself had wanted to take Lucia only as far as Cádiz and have her make the rest of the journey overland, and it was only at her father's express wish that he had agreed to travel so far up the straits of Gibraltar. He somehow had the feeling that it would be worth his while to learn a little more about this Captain Maynard.

Garnet had not moved from her position in the middle of the bright, deep carpet. She heard the door open and soft footsteps coming towards her but she stared downwards, making an effort to stop herself trembling.

Sulimary Ali was not alone. A short, fat man dressed in colourful robes stood looking at her, his small eyes shrewdly probing.

'Take off the veil,' Sulimary Ali said in a deceptively soft voice, and Garnet obeyed him. He lifted a lock of her hair and rubbed it between his fingers.

'You see, the girl has charm, do you not agree?' Ali stepped back. 'She is too thin and small for a wife or even for the bed but she might make some entertainment for us.'

He caught Garnet's shoulder. 'You can dance, girl, isn't that so?'

She nodded quickly. She would do anything he wanted so long as she did not have to lie with him.

'You see.' Ali lifted his hand. 'Shall we have her at our auction and let her serve the food and then perform her little dance for us?'

The man nodded slowly. 'Perhaps. But she is pale and weak. I do not see her being of much interest.'

'You are wrong, Abdul.' Sulimary's voice had an edge to it. 'She is at least a little better than your never-ending procession of snake charmers. Yes, my mind is made up. I shall allow her to dance and then I shall sell her to whomsoever will offer me a good price.'

Abdul shrugged thick shoulders. 'I should get rid of her as quickly as possible,' he said. 'She will only become more thin and ugly as she grows older.'

'Ah, then you will not want her for your bed to-night?' the sultan said quietly. 'I am disappointed in you, Abdul. I thought you would admire the wench.' He turned to Garnet impatiently.

'Go back to the seraglio and tell Marhabba you do not please me. She shall send me one of my wives and a bondservant for Abdul. A woman with more meat on her bones, eh, my friend?'

The man nodded eagerly, turning to Garnet. 'I like dark skin, you see girl.' He spread his arms wide. 'Do not be downcast, perhaps you will appeal to one of the guests your master invites into his home.' He turned to Sulimary Ali. 'Though I can't think of any man who would not rather one of our own women.'

The sultan's mouth curved downwards as he stared sullenly at Garnet. 'To think I gave a valuable gold brooch set with rubies for her. I must have been crazed by the sun.' He pushed her roughly. 'Go on, get out of my sight.'

The eunuch was outside the door waiting, his arms folded across his great chest. He gave her a look of sympathy, knowing that she had failed to find favour in her master's sight.

As she walked along beside him, Garnet's heart was beating swiftly. She was thankful to have escaped so lightly from the presence of the sultan and his ugly friend. She was grateful that she was too thin and too pale. Perhaps now Ali might allow her to go free. He had talked of her dancing before his friends, but perhaps in view of Abdul's doubt about the soundness of the idea, Sulimary Ali might forget it entirely.

Marhabba laughed loud and long when she heard of Garnet's disgrace. Her chins wobbled against the neck of her chemise and she flicked her whip against the white girl's arm more in humour than anger. She listened to the eunuch's orders that a wife and another bondservant be sent to the master and she rolled about even more, almost falling from the stool upon which she was crouched like a large fat spider.

Garnet was forgotten then as the women began quarrelling amongst themselves. It seemed they all wanted the honour of being taken to Sulimary Ali's bed.

She stood against the wall and closed her eyes for a moment, her relief disappearing and a terrible hopelessness taking its place. She might not be in danger of becoming the sultan's favourite any more, but she was still within the strong high walls of the seraglio, perhaps doomed to remain there all her life.

She lifted her head. Unless she danced so well that one of the men bought her. At least when she was taken away from the barren rocky fortress, she would stand some chance of escape.

To achieve her aim, she would have to make friends with the kadin. She it was who allocated tasks to the bondservants. If Garnet could persuade her to allow her to dance, perhaps even to show her the intricate movements, she would find favour with one of Ali's guests. After what he had said about her, he would be only too eager to sell her to anyone who was interested.

The eunuch was sitting down on a pile of cushions, helping himself to a plate of sweetmeats. He was bored with the quarrels of the wives, he had seen them often before.

Garnet crossed the soft carpet, aware that if Marhabba saw her, she would be immediately sent back to the kitchens. She crouched down beside the large blackamoor and looked up at him pleadingly.

'Will you help me?' she asked. He stared down at her in bewilderment, his large eyes rolling in his head. He was not used to being spoken to as though he was a person with feelings.

'What you want?' he said suspiciously. 'I have nothing, no gold or jewels, how can I help you?'

Garnet had been busy plucking at the gems sewn onto her waistcoat. She handed him one and his face creased into a broad smile.

'All I want is for Marhabba to teach me to dance before the sultan,' she said softly. 'I do not wish to be a disgrace yet again.'

She twisted another stone from the edge of the small garment and the eunuch's large hand closed around it. He shook his head and made a wry face.

'Marhabba, she is bad-tempered one,' he said doubtfully. 'I don't know what to say, make her listen to me.'

'Tell her the sultan will be eternally grateful to her,' Garnet suggested breathlessly. 'Tell her he wishes to sell me but I have no value unless I can dance. You know she hates me, she would do anything to be rid of me.'

He was still doubtful, pulling at the tassels in the plump cushion at his side.

'The kadin will always remember your help,' she said softly. 'She will give you the best bits from the table and perhaps she may even reward you with jewels or gold if the sultan is pleased by the money I bring him at the sale.'

'Very well, I will try.' The large man lumbered to his feet and crossed the carpeted floor, pushing aside the flimsy drapes behind which the women chosen to go to their master were being prepared.

Marhabba's voice, loud and penetrating, filled the large room, ringing through the criss-cross patterns of the windows, echoing down the long corridors outside. She came marching solidly towards where Garnet stood, her whip raised. Garnet braced herself, waiting for the blow to fall, but the kadin stopped for a moment, her broad forehead creased in a frown. Slowly, she let her arm fall to her side and then, after a moment, she nodded.

She pulled Garnet forward into the small antichamber at the side of the larger room. She closed the door and stared at Garnet's thin frame, shaking her head doubtfully. With a sigh, she drew off her long chemise so that her massive waist was exposed. She lifted her arms and, with unexpected grace, began to dance, her hips moving swiftly from side to side. The beads hanging from her neck shivered and gleamed and Garnet glimpsed the beautiful woman the kadin had once been.

She stopped at last, her face beaded with perspiration and she nodded to Garnet, pushing at her arm, urging her to attempt the intricate dance. Slowly at first, with self-conscious jerking of her hips, Garnet began to move. Marhabba, her face tight with concentration, prodded her with the flat end of the whip and shook her head. Again, she demonstrated the correct way of shaking her hip and stomach and, with a great effort of will, Garnet tried again.

It was almost an hour later, when the eunuch brought a tray of iced sugar water, that Marhabba fell onto a flurry of cushions, her face red with exertion. She sipped her drink and spoke to the ungainly blackamoor who smiled down at Garnet encouragingly.

'The kadin say you get better,' he said quickly. 'If you have lessons again tomorrow and the day after and perhaps for the rest of week you be one of best dancers in seraglio.'

Garnet took a long drink of the sugared water and smiled at Marhabba and, after a momentary hesitation, the kadin inclined her head in acknowledgement of the new bond of mutual respect that had grown up between them.

CHAPTER EIGHTEEN

Life became more pleasant for Garnet in the seraglio as the kadin continued to teach her to dance. Marhabba's enthusiasm for her task increased as she found that the white woman was a quick and apt pupil and would follow her instructions with untiring resolve. This woman from the West might be thin and pale but beneath her delicate exterior there was courage and endurance and, almost against her will, Marhabba began to feel a fondness for her.

Instead of giving Garnet the most menial tasks, she excused her from kitchen duties entirely, enjoying her role as pedagogue so much that she took her instructions beyond the dancing lessons and taught the girl how to bow correctly before her betters. Marhabba would be almost sorry to see the white one leave the seraglio but she was determined that she would give her the best possible chance of being sold to a man of worth and quality.

She had coaxed the girl into eating a little more of the richly spiced food that she herself was so fond of and, indeed, the effect was as she had hoped. Garnet began to fill out, her thin frame was more rounded, her breasts full and yet firm. She was still too thin and small by Eastern standards but an improvement there certainly was.

Marhabba had ordered the seamstress to make an entire wardrobe of clothes for the English girl and, even though she said it herself, her choice of colours had been brilliant. The green and gold silk and the soft white muslin enhanced the beautiful red hair which in the kadin's opinion was the only redeeming quality Garnet possessed in the way of beauty.

As for Garnet herself, she found she was recovering her spirits now that she had a set purpose in mind. She learned quickly, knowing that her one opportunity of escaping from the seraglio was to catch the eye of another master, someone who of necessity would have travelled far to enjoy Sulimary Ali's hospitality. She would pretend to be docile, a willing servant, but when she saw the slightest chance of running away, she would take it.

She was on her way to the kadin's chambers now, though she knew there was little more she could learn. She had come to understand some of what Marhabba said to her, picking up a word of her language here and there. When the two women wished to communicate more fully, the big black eunuch was sent for and he acted as interpreter. He was with the kadin when Garnet bowed her way into the chambers and, with a sinking of her heart, she realized that the moment had come when she must put all she had learned into practice.

Fez smiled at her widely, his teeth gleaming against his black skin. With a quick look in Marhabba's direction, he began to speak.

'The kadin wish me to tell you that you perform before the master tonight; it is to show him what you have accomplished.' He nodded his great head. 'Marhabba, she put a word in master's ear, she tell him how excellent is your learning of the dance.'

Garnet hid her feeling of nervousness and smiled her thanks at the kadin who spoke rapidly to Fez.

'You must not dance this morning, it good to rest and prepare yourself and you must not eat greatly, the food will make you heavy on your feet.' He grinned and his eyes went to Marhabba's great bulk as though in warning to Garnet.

'Tell the kadin that I thank her for all she has done for me,' Garnet said softly. 'I shall not fail her.'

Marhabba clapped her hands loudly and two of the bondservants glided as if from nowhere, eyes downcast, waiting for the great wife of the sultan to speak. She gave her orders in a harsh voice with much flicking of her horse-hair whip and then, with waving movement of her huge arms, ushered them all from her room.

'Kadin say she can teach you nothing more,' Fez said to Garnet. 'Now you must excel yourself, otherwise master not allow you to dance before his guests.' Fez was silent for a moment. 'The truth is, he sorry he bought you, he wish to sell you and, if he do not, you will feel his anger.'

'I know,' Garnet said. 'Don't worry about me, Fez, I shall be all right.'

The big man followed the bondservants as they led Garnet towards the scented, heated waters of the baths. He sat cross-legged at the side of the steps, eating jelly pieces from a small bag tied to his waist. His large silk pantaloons spread around his legs in soft colourful folds and his body glistened with scented oil. He smiled his encouragement as Garnet was disrobed and taken into the steaming baths.

Garnet closed her eyes as the water lapped around her. She was reminded once more of Jonathon Summers' house and of Wolfe and her heart missed a beat. She could not deny that she still loved her husband, although she had long since accepted that he had no feeling at all for her. And yet, as they had stood side by side being joined together in marriage, she had truly believed they would be happy. What a naïve fool she had been. Wolfe was a law unto himself, he needed no one, not Lucia, not Jonathon and certainly not herself.

The bondservants were washing her long hair with spicy, scented herbs. Their hands were soft and gentle, they treated her as though she was a kadin, not a humble slave as they were. She felt sorry for them; they would never know anything but the high, imprisoning walls of the seraglio. They would be slaves for the rest of their lives, not even given the occasional honour of lying with their lord.

But she was different, she was not content to remain in servitude for a moment longer than was necessary She would dance her heart out and convince Ali that she was worthy to entertain his guests.

She had heard him speak of an auction and she was

curious about what would take place. It was all done with great ceremony, that much was clear by the way the sultan had talked to his friend Abdul. Possibly other rich, powerful men of the country came from miles around to attend such a gathering. Garnet smiled to herself. Perhaps Fez could help her learn a little more about the visitors; one who lived in the vicinity of Tangiers would be very useful.

The bondservants had finished their task of washing her hair and were splashing about in the water like children, laughing delightedly as the black kohl ran in streaks along their faces. Garnet smiled indulgently as she climbed up the steps and immediately the girls followed her, wrapping her in long bright towels.

Carefully, she was patted dry and one of the bondservants brought her new garments given Garnet by the kadin. The pantaloons were of silk gauze, wide at the ankle but drawn in by a circlet of gold and jewels. The smock was tiny, created especially to reveal Garnet's breasts to the best advantage. The kadin, considering her to be lacking in quantity of flesh, wished to enhance the slight charms she possessed.

The waistcoat was brief, fitting at the waist and encrusted with myriads of tiny pearls. Bracelets of gold and silver set with rubies and pearls were placed upon Garnet's arms and a cap of silk upon her head.

Garnet realized she was far more richly attired than she had been when she last visited the sultan, but now she had the approval of Marhabba to aid her.

She looked up to see Fez watching her with large eyes. He smiled, nodding his great head even as he popped a sweetmeat into his mouth. He rose to his feet, his arms folded, waiting for the signal that she was ready.

One of the bondservants spoke to him softly and he moved forward, his shoulders bent as he leaned towards Garnet.

'We shall go to wait the master's pleasure,' he said smiling. 'He will like the white girl when he see her, she very beautiful now.'

He moved through the lace hangings and led the way along the now familiar corridors until he opened the huge door. The carpets were rich and deep along the passageways and great chandeliers sent shivers of light darting into the gloom. Fez took Garnet to an arched doorway and paused for a moment.

'We are to wait in the vestibule of the fountains,' he said. 'It is there you will be allowed to dance before the great sultan. I wish you the smiles of the gods and pray the evil one turns his face from you.'

The room was one Garnet had never seen before. Scarlet and cream tiles covered the floor and the walls were patterned with an intricate design of coloured stones.

Set into one of the walls was a small fountain, the sparkling water running into a deep basin of bronze decorated with the heads of eagles that poured water from cruel-looking beaks.

Garnet twisted her hands together nervously as she watched Fez seat himself on a pile of cushions. He smiled at her, beckoning with his great hand.

'Sit for a while,' he said. 'The sultan might not see

you for a long time.'

She sat beside him, careful not to crease the gauze pantaloons. She felt cold and frightened and wondered if she could possibly remember all that Marhabba had taught her.

'Tell me about yourself, Fez,' she said to the eunuch. 'How did you come to be in the seraglio of Sulimary Ali?'

He reached into the bag at his side and popped a sweetmeat into his mouth, chewing consideringly before answering.

'I am a Sandali,' he said at last. 'That mean shaved clean of vital parts.'

Garnet stared at him. She had not meant to pry but, once Fez had begun to talk, it seemed he did not want to stop.

'As child, I chosen for my size.' He chewed another sweetmeat as though considering the honour that had been done him. He smiled. 'I plump boy, large of arm and chest, so I taken and made into eunuch for the sultan.' His face was pensive.

'It greatly painful, a sharp razor cuts and then wound cauterized with boiling oil. Then I place in dung hill and fed on only milk. Some boys die, but I strong and live.' He flexed his large arms and Garnet saw the muscles rippling beneath the dark skin.

Garnet stared at him in pitying amazement. She had grown used to the sight of eunuchs sitting around whilst the women of the seraglio bathed or dressed themselves, not pausing to wonder why these men were allowed to look upon the wives of the sultan with impunity. He caught her expression and smiled at her widely.

'I do not mind,' he said. 'I am always so, I know nothing else. I have comfortable life and do not need to labour under the heat of the sun. Do not be sorry, little white lady.'

Garnet touched his hand lightly for a moment. 'Fez, I need your help,' she said. 'I would like you to learn about the visitors who come to the auction. Please, try to find out if there is one from Tangiers.'

He shrugged. 'I will talk to the servants who wait upon the master. They hear gossip and in exchange for some token they will tell me what they know.'

Garnet smiled and pointed to the jewel-encrusted bracelets on her arm.

'I do not think Marhabba would notice if one or two of these were to disappear,' she said softly.

Fez put a warning finger to his lips, rising to his feet quickly, standing to attention, arms folded across his great chest.

Sulimary Ali swept into the vestibule, his robes flowing around his feet, his eyes dark as they looked upon Garnet. She scrambled to a standing position, waiting for instructions from the sultan.

He gestured impatiently for her to come nearer and, with his hand grasping her arm, he turned her around slowly, his gaze critical.

'You do not look so thin and pale,' he said. 'Marhabba do well. But, I will see you perform, I will not look the fool before my guests. You dance for me now.'

There were no pipes or drums but Garnet, used to practising with the kadin without music, lifted her arms gracefully and placed her feet in such a position that her weight was balanced, allowing her to move her body rapidly whilst remaining in the same spot.

She was aware of Sulimary's amazement as her hips gyrated, sending the pearls on her waistcoat fluttering and spinning as though they had a life of their own.

She leaped into the air then and turned away from Ali, performing a series of intricate steps so swiftly that the gold at her ankles sent out sparks of light. She felt triumphant, knowing that she excelled herself, putting all that Marhabba had taught her and more into the dance. She spun before the sultan, her hair flying outwards, and one glimpse at his face told her that he was impressed.

As she swept past Fez, he gave her a wink, though his face remained impassive. Garnet spun and weaved, shaking her hips and stomach to a rhythm that she heard inside her head. It was as though long buried instincts had risen up to come to her aid, putting spirit and life into her movements.

At last, she fell breathless at Sulimary Ali's feet, her hair hanging over her face, her breasts heaving from her exertions.

He spoke to her, his voice revealing his sense of satisfaction. 'Yes, you shall dance for me at the auction. I think I shall manage to sell you, after all.'

When Garnet looked up at him, it was to see that he was actually smiling. He took her hand and raised her to her feet and, from within the folds of his robe, he took a pouch.

'Here,' he handed it to her. 'It is a reward for your efforts. I have heard how you have worked to please me. This small gift is a token of my regard and, though I do not find you pleasing enough for my bed, I think you will find one among my guests who may think you quite beautiful.'

He spoke to Fez rapidly in his own language and, without looking at Garnet again, left the room. As the door shut behind him, Garnet peered into the pouch of leather that he had given her. It contained a gold and silver necklace, with dark green flashing emeralds set into the intricate patterning.

'I have succeeded, Fez,' Garnet said happily. 'I am to dance at the auction, did you hear?' Her heart was beating rapidly, she was still breathless with excitement. There was hope for her now, the prospect of leaving the dark stone fortress set upon the rocky cliffs for ever. In her excitement, she did not notice at first that Fez was unsmiling. He bowed his head as he led her from the vestibule and she had to run to catch up with him.

'Fez,' she said as her feet tripped lightly over the rich carpet of the corridor leading from the sultan's apartments. 'Fez, wait, what's wrong?'

He turned and looked down at her in the gloom from the flickering chandeliers. His round face wore a sombre expression and his dark eyes refused to meet hers.

She caught his arm and looked up at him. 'What did

Sulimary Ali say to you, please tell me. It concerns my future, doesn't it?'

Slowly, he nodded. 'A man comes to the auction. One who buys women for evil purposes.'

'Tell me.' Garnet's lips were stiff. 'What do you mean, Fez? I have to know.'

Fez walked on in silence, his big shoulders slumped. Garnet hurried after him, her mind racing over what he had said. What could the eunuch mean by evil purposes?

As they neared the large bolted door, Garnet stopped running behind Fez. She stood quite still, staring at his retreating back. At last he turned.

'I am going no further until you explain to me what has upset you,' she said quietly. 'Once we are back in the seraglio, there will be other women and you won't have the chance to talk with me privately.'

He looked at her, his large dark eyes sad. 'You are to dance before a man who keeps a house of ill repute,' he said. 'Men will be able to buy your services for a few pieces of silver.'

CHAPTER NINETEEN

It had been a blow at first, Garnet conceded to herself, to know that she might be bought by the owner of a bawdy house. Later, however, when she stopped to consider the matter, she realized she was no worse off than she had been before. Her plan was still to escape from her new master, whoever he might be.

She became caught up in the excitement of the seraglio as preparations for the forthcoming auction reached their zenith. Even Marhabba forgot to use her whip on the bondservants and became almost amiable.

From the kitchens wafted the aroma of succulent stews rich with mutton, and great pots of pilaw were kept warm near the fireside. Trays of sugared fruits were arranged along the tables, the bright colours glittering in the sunshine from the windows.

Garnet found a moment in all the excitement to talk with Fez, presenting him with one of her bracelets in exchange for information.

'The man who wishes to see you,' Fez said in a low voice, 'is a white man, very rich so it is said. He wears much golden jewellery and his clothes are of the finest.'

'Where is he from?' Garnet asked anxiously, and Fez's white teeth showed in a smile.

'Only a short way from the harbour at Tangiers. This is what you wanted to know.' He put his head on one side. 'But why is this important?'

Garnet was cautious. 'I have friends a short distance from there, Fez.' It was better that he knew as little as possible, she mused. After her disappearance, he might be questioned, and she would not like him to be punished for his assistance.

Fez tucked the bracelet into the band of silk at his waist. He rose to his feet slowly.

'This payment is not for me,' he said. 'I would take nothing from you. It is demanded by the servant of the sultan, you understand.'

'I know, Fez.' Garnet smiled up at the huge man. 'I am grateful to you.' She watched him leave the chamber, walking softly on his bare feet. She had made friends of the eunuch and of the kadin, too, the unlikeliest companions she had ever known.

Marhabba approached her, holding a cap of silk in her plump hands, indicating by the way of signs that she wished Garnet to pin it to her henna'd hair. The kadin was a vain woman, dyeing away the grey that showed her maturity with the red dye that was an extract from a leaf brought from Cyprus. She used the dye to cover her nails and the extremities of her feet as well as for the shaved pubes beneath her large stomach. She remained still as Garnet pinned the cap into place and clapped her hands in delight at the result.

She smiled up at Garnet, her hands on her huge hips. She spoke slowly in halting English, as pleased as a child with her accomplishment.

'I wish you well,' she stumbled a little over the words. 'For tonight, you dance.'

Garnet felt a dart of fear, nervous now that the festivities were imminent. She forced herself to smile at Marhabba and bow her head in acknowledgement of the honour the kadin had done her, in learning a few words of her language.

One of the other eunuchs came before Marhabba and spoke to her in a low voice. The kadin frowned, letting forth a stream of abuse, her dark eyes flashing. The man shrugged, his hands spread outwards, palms facing up as though disclaiming any responsibility. At last Marhabba shook her head and made a sweeping gesture with her hands. The eunuch bowed to Garnet and stood back, waiting for her to go with him.

At Garnet's questioning glance, the kadin shook her head again and moved away, towards the bond-servant holding a tray of iced water and sugared delights. There seemed nothing that Garnet could do but go with the man, though she did not like the way he looked at her. She instinctively felt a mistrust of the eunuch that she could not explain even to herself.

She was dressed in clean, fresh pantaloons and a loose smock of pale blue silk. Not the exotic garments expected of one who was to visit the sultan. And yet she was being led to Sulimary Ali's quarters; it was very puzzling.

In the vestibule of the fountain, she saw Abdul, his fat face wreathed in smiles as he leaned back against the great mound of silk cushions.

She stood before him waiting for him to speak and he stared at her in open curiosity, his fingers picking at a bowl of fruit set on the small polished table beside him.

'What is it you want?' Garnet asked, and Abdul heaved himself to his knees, his chins quivering. He waved his hand to the eunuch and, with a respectful bow, the man withdrew, closing the door firmly behind him.

Garnet was uneasy. She watched as Abdul stumbled to his feet. His breath smelled strongly of herb beer and his eyes were blurred and blood shot.

'Dance,' he said, his speech slurred and indistinct. 'I have heard how wonderful you are and I wish to see for myself.'

Garnet backed away as the man came towards her. She stood against the cool of the wall, her hands spread against the coloured stones.

'Where is the sultan?' she asked suspiciously. 'Does he know you've sent for me?' She turned her face away as Abdul leaned towards her, smiling foolishly.

'I am in command here, white one,' he said thickly. 'And when I say to dance I do not expect a refusal.'

He caught her wrist and twisted her arm cruelly, the smile still on his lips. Garnet realized that, in spite of the man's bulk and his apparent state of intoxication, he was dangerous.

'Very well.' She pulled away from him quickly. 'I shall dance for you, if that is what you wish.' She lifted her arms and spun away from him and he staggered as he tried to follow her.

She moved her hips rapidly, her smock whispering against her skin. She was not properly dressed for the occasion, a fact which did not escape Abdul's fuddled mind.

'Wait,' he called harshly, and as Garnet paused for breath, the man came towards her, his hands outstretched. He caught the soft silk of her smock and tore it away from her, laughing at the look of outrage that flickered across her face.

'That is more fitting, though you have the most tiny breasts I have ever seen.' He laughed again without mirth, his eyes cold and cruel.

She began to dance away from him, feeling that it was best that she keep moving. She hoped fervently that someone would come and interrupt the proceedings. She felt sure that Sulimary Ali was not aware of what was going on beneath his roof.

But after a while she began to tire. Abdul had settled himself back against the cushion with the expression of a wild beast about to pounce on its prey. Garnet was forced to pause in her dancing and Abdul smiled spitefully.

'Come to me,' he commanded loudly. Garnet cautiously moved a little closer and he reached out, catching her long hair between his fingers, tugging at the silken strands, forcing her to kneel beside him.

'I have never had a white woman.' He ran his fingers along her breasts, tweaking at the rosy nipple, laughing when Garnet winced with pain. 'You are so delicate, a piece of porcelain, perhaps I should buy you from my friend before the auction begins.'

Garnet tried to move away, but Abdul held her fast, drawing her head backwards, his moist mouth moving to her throat and downwards to her breasts. She shuddered, trying to control the feeling of panic that swept through her.

'My lord might not wish to sell me to you,' she gasped. 'He has someone else in mind.'

Abdul pressed her down among the bed of cushions, his hands on the waistband of silk that held her pantaloons.

'I know about that. Would you rather live in a house where many men could use your sweet flesh than belong to Abdul?'

She remained silent, not wishing to anger him. In his muddled state of mind, he could do anything. She gasped as he tore away the silk garment from her waist. He stared at her nakedness, licking his lips, his eyes wide.

'So white, so perfectly made,' he said in a whisper. 'I must have you, just this once my pretty. Say nothing to Sulimary Ali and I will make you rich.'

Garnet gasped with relief. The knowledge that he was attacking her without the sultan's consent made it easier for her to fight him. She relaxed under his grasp as though agreeing to his demands. He cupped her breast with a fat hand, pushing his knee between her legs.

As he fumbled beneath his robes, she pushed him with all her strength and he fell back against the marble tiles, an expression of astonishment on his face.

She looked around her wildly for something with which to defend herself. Hanging against the wall was a curved sword in a scarlet and gold scabbard. Garnet rushed towards it and Abdul reached out clutching fingers that caught at her ankles, bringing her down heavily beside him. He laughed harshly and rolled towards her, slapping her face lightly, his face sneering as he looked down at her.

'It will do no good to struggle, you only excite me further. I will have you, so be still and allow me to have my enjoyment of you.'

He reared up above her and Garnet screamed out, loud and long in terror and despair. Abdul was taken by surprise and, for a moment, his hold on her shoulders relaxed and she wriggled away from him. This time she reached her objective. She plucked the sword from the wall and held it before her, pointing it at Abdul's throat.

From behind her, she heard the scurry of footsteps, hands came around her, relieving her of her weapon. She turned her head and looked into the angry face of the sultan. He thrust her aside and stared down at the drawn face of Abdul, quivering now with fear.

'You bedan!' Sulimary Ali said in a low voice. 'You violate the privacy of my seraglio by having one of my own women brought to you. Imbecile. Did you think you could get away with such an act?'

'But the white one, you wish to sell her, I buy, I give you much gold, anything you want,' Abdul was whining, his fat face moist with perspiration.

'Silence.' The sultan issued an order and two burly guards entered the chamber, catching Abdul in a powerful grip and dragging him screaming from the room. He was calling Sulimary Ali, over and over again, his voice hysterical with fear. At last the sound of his protests died away into silence and Garnet turned to the sultan, her hands clenched together in fear.

'What will happen to him?' she asked in a whisper, and Sulimary Ali stared at her with cold eyes.

'He will die for his betrayal of our friendship,' he said. 'What part did you have to play in this little scheme, woman?' He placed the sword back into the scabbard and waited, arms crossed in front of him for her to reply.

'I know nothing,' she said. 'One of the eunuchs came for me and, though Marhabba did not understand, she was obliged to send me to your apartments.'

He was looking her over carefully and Garnet was acutely aware of her nakedness. She bent and retrieved a torn piece of her smock, attempting to cover herself.

'Do not be afraid,' he said. 'I do not want you.' He grinned. 'It amused me to buy you and now the story of your adventure with Abdul will bring a great deal of curiosity. There will be much interest shown when you dance before my guests tonight.' He turned away from her.

'Go, back to the seraglio. Have the women prepare you. Let Marhabba herself robe you in the richest garments from my store and the finest jewels she can lay her hands upon.'

He turned his back on her and the exchange between them was obviously over. He left the vestibule of the fountains, his robes fluttering behind him, calling orders to his servants.

To Garnet's relief, it was Fez who came to return her to the seraglio. He looked down into her face, his shrewd eyes missing nothing of her torn clothes or the scratches on her pale skin.

'That man Abdul, I never trusted him,' he said. 'He come round looking through windows of seraglio and I feel like throwing hot oil into his eyes.'

'Why did you not tell Marhabba?' Garnet asked, and Fez shrugged his large shoulders.

'It not my place to tell about coming and going of master's guests.' He smiled. 'But fat pig get more than oil in his face now.'

He unbolted the door and, as Garnet reached the perfumed rooms of the seraglio, a babble of feminine voices greeted her. Marhabba came towards her, eyes wide with shock. She shook her head, talking swiftly, and Garnet listened helplessly, understanding nothing of what the kadin said.

'She angry that Abdul make fool of her,' Fez explained. 'Kadin wish she could plunge dagger in his heart as you tried to do.'

Garnet was amazed that the story of her exploits had spread so quickly. It seemed the women thought her a heroine for repulsing the man's advances. It was unheard of for any other person than the sultan himself to lay a finger on any of the women of the seraglio without his express orders.

Bowls of hot, scented water were placed near Garnet's feet and one of the bondservants began to wash her, with slow gentle movements of her hands. Marhabba offered her a long glass of sugared water and removed the tattered remnants of her clothes, clucking her tongue in sympathy as she saw the marks made by Abdul as he'd fought with Garnet.

The kadin sat beside her, instructing Fez to question Garnet, listening in awe as the eunuch recounted what had happened when the white one had stepped into the vestibule of the fountains and found not her master but the fat, evil Abdul. Garnet, watching the faces of the women, wondered if the eunuch was embroidering the tale. At any rate, there were a great many sighs of wonder as he talked.

She saw by the way Fez swung his large hands that
for shopping with us e sword. She could
e remembered the
e blade, her hands
at would have hap-
vened.
ez and he listened,
. At last he smiled
been said.
that you may keep
id you are honour-
eing thin and ugly.

She love you as though you were her own daughter.'
He rose to his feet. 'You must rest now, while I stand
guard. You must be refreshed and strong for the
festivities tonight.'

In the large chamber with soft curtains of silk gauze
fluttering over the arched windows, Garnet lay back
against an array of bright silk cushions and closed her
eyes. She knew that Fez stood outside her door, determined that she should not be disturbed from her
rest by anyone. And she needed to sleep; she had to
renew her strength for whatever lay before her at the
auction. Her mind must be clear when she was sold to
her new master. She sighed softly and, in spite of her
brave intentions to escape, she knew, deep within her,
that she was afraid.

Wolfe was smiling as he was led into the small stuffy
cabin. The captain sat on a chair, gesturing towards a
bottle of rum, and when his guest shook his head, he
helped himself to a liberal measure, standing the glass
of deep dark liquor on the table before him.

'Now, dear sir, what can I do for you?' He rubbed
his hands together incessantly, his small beady eyes
alight with avarice as he took in every detail of the
Englishman's appearance. There might be rich pick-
ings here if he played the game with his usual cunning.

Wolfe controlled his anger. 'I am looking for a
woman. She is easy to recognize, she has flame-
coloured hair.' He spoke calmly, as one reasonable
man to another, though he longed to place his hands
round the fat captain's throat.

'Let me see now, have I heard anything about this lady? I'm not sure.'

Wolfe leaned back in his chair, a smile on his lips as he saw Maynard begin to sweat.

'Let me refresh your memory,' he said softly. 'You have dealings with one Sulimary Ali, I believe. There is a brisk trade between the two of you in property that does not, strictly speaking, belong to you.'

The captain had become pale. He took a quick gulp from his glass, desperately trying to ascertain how much the Englishman really knew.

'My dear sir, I'm not sure I understand your meaning,' he said at last. He mopped his face with his bright kerchief, cursing himself for allowing the man on board his ship. But he still had the upper hand, he could call his crew at any moment and have the fellow forcibly ejected.

'Perhaps you would like to expand on what you were saying?' He felt a little more confident now. What could his countryman do after all?

Wolfe moved towards him, towering above the captain as he shrank back in his chair.

'Very well.' He folded his arms across his broad chest. 'You have traded in carbines and other naval property.' He smiled. 'Do not bother to make a denial. I have witnesses who will attest to the fact.'

He walked slowly around the cabin, picking up a chart and studying it with apparent lack of concern.

'What do you want of me?' Captain Maynard took another drink from his glass and his hand shook.

'The girl. Where is she?' He put down the chart and

flexed his fingers, his face set, his eyes cold.

'Very well,' Maynard said quickly. 'Sit down, dear chap, and I will try to explain.'

Wolfe remained standing, controlling his impatience. Let the man first tell him all he wanted to know and then he could allow himself the satisfaction of smashing his fist into Maynard's sweating face.

CHAPTER TWENTY

Garnet stood arrayed in all her finery, waiting for the summons to the sultan's presence. She held her head aloft under the jewel-encrusted cap and the lace veil fluttered around her face as she sighed.

The women had taken the best part of two hours to prepare her, painting her eyes with kohl, darkening the outer edges and thickening her eyebrows. Her nails were scarlet with dye and it had taken all Garnet's powers of persuasion to prevent Marhabba from shaving the small triangle of golden hair beneath the flat planes of her stomach and daubing the red dye there too.

Fez came and stood in the doorway, his head bowed meekly as he spoke to Marhabba. The kadin nodded and fluffed out the veil, tweaking the beads around Garnet's waist into place before stepping back, her head on one side as she smiled in satisfaction.

She paused for a moment as Garnet waited for instructions and then, on an impulse, hugged the slight figure of the white girl to her ample bosom.

Fez was grinning as he led Garnet along the corridor. 'You be most beautiful lady in auction,' he said. 'I don't care if kadin think you thin and ugly, I think you pretty.'

Garnet glanced up at him. 'Will there be other women at the auction, Fez?' she asked in surprise. The eunuch nodded vigorously.

'Yes, from other seraglios. They ones master grow tired of, wish to sell or exchange for other women. You the only one from here, Sulimary Ali like to keep his wives and bondservants, to show how powerful and rich he is.'

He took her through a doorway that was unfamiliar to her and she looked along the corridor to where a large chamber opened up before them.

'That is royal saloon,' Fez explained. 'Soon, all the visitors come there to eat and drink after sale. You must wait there to be called out into the courtyard. I stay with you.'

The saloon was high, with a domed, painted ceiling. Great arched alcoves were hung with heavy drapes, concealing scrolled, gilt sofas. It was to one of these that Fez led her.

He himself stood at attention, arms folded, his muscles bulging. He nodded his encouragement as Garnet seated herself, careful not to crush the silk of her pantaloons.

'I will miss you, white lady,' Fez said in a low voice. 'You have been my only friend. No one like eunuch, not man not woman, we like carpet under feet.' He gave a long sigh and was silent for a moment.

'Perhaps, one day, I become the kisla agha, that is

chief of all eunuchs, then I be happy.'

Garnet stared at his broad, shining back and, slowly, she unclasped the pendant given her by Sulimary Ali when she had danced for him.

'Here, take it,' she said. 'It will be more use to you than to me. It is the only jewel from all I wear now that is truly mine and I want you to have it, Fez.'

His large eyes were wide as he saw the glittering gold lie in his fingers. His smile was wide, like a child's, as he tucked the gift into his waistband.

The outer door was opened suddenly and a uniformed halberdier gestured imperiously to Fez. He gave a command in a gutteral voice and the eunuch looked down at Garnet.

'It is time,' he said slowly. 'You must go, we will not meet again.'

He stood back as Garnet made her way to where the sun streamed into the saloon from the wide courtyard outside. She heard him cough, as though at any moment he might begin to cry, and she hurried away from him, not trusting her own emotions.

The noise and heat and the rich, ripe smell of fruit greeted Garnet as she stepped outside. For a moment, she could not see, so bright was the sun after the gloom of the saloon. Then her eyes became accustomed to the light and she saw that the courtyard in the sultan's seraglio was similar to a market place in Tangiers.

Pipers sat cross-legged on colourful mats, a long basket containing snakes set before them. Traders had brought a variety of goods to sell, from small trinkets of copper to huge sacks of brightly coloured spices.

Against one of the walls was a dais and, upon it, a young negress. Her slender body was gleaming with oil and around her, as she stood unselfconsciously, almost uncaring, the bidding was going on.

It was conducted in a desultory fashion with none of the men very eager to make the purchase. The girl would be used only as a servant for the heavier work of the seraglio such as the scrubbing of floors and washing of long, dusty walls.

Garnet was taken towards where Sulimary Ali sat upon a high platform, a canopy spread over his head. She saw him look her over in appraisal before, apparently satisfied, he commanded her to sit at his feet.

'I have kept you as the last item on the list,' he said flatly. 'You will be the highlight of the auction because, so far, no one has shown a great deal of interest in my sale. The women have been mostly hags, or too young for any use. But you will salve my pride. Already looks are coming your way.'

Garnet hung her head. The heat of the sun beat down on her and she forced herself to be calm. She would not stay long with her new master, whoever he might be.

The negress was led from the stand and Garnet closed her eyes, trying to find the courage for the ordeal that was to come. She rose as the halberdier took her arm, walking her slowly across the heat of the courtyard and towards the dais.

She stood head erect, arms to her sides. There was a feeling of tension among the onlookers now; even the snake charmers forgot to pipe out their sweet haunting music. The veil was lifted from Garnet's face and, in the silence, a voice rang out. 'Don't just stand there, woman, let us see you dance.'

The drums began to beat with a loud bold sound and Garnet stood for a moment in silence. She lifted her arms above her head then, knowing that Marhabba would be blamed if her performance was not all that Sulimary Ali expected. Her steps were hesitant at first, but then she closed her eyes to the staring faces of the men, leaning forward now, eagerly watching.

Her mind rose as free as a bird, above the walls of the seraglio. She lay again in her husband's arms, savouring the moments of love between them. Everything had been so wonderful before she had realized that he still cared about Lucia more than he cared for anything else in the world.

She thought of his arms around her, holding her close, of his mouth, warm and demanding upon hers. It was impossible, and yet she knew she still loved him, in spite of everything he had done, in spite of his many betrayals.

She danced as though all her sorrow and longing were poured into the movements of her body. She found a skill she had not known she possessed. She whirled faster as the drums beat more loudly, inside her head, in time with her heartbeats. She was possessed by the music, oblivious of the silent men watching her with awe. With a loud roll, the drumming ceased and the dance was over. Garnet sank down onto the ground, her arms stretched out behind her, her long slender neck arching backwards, her hair hanging in the dust.

After a moment, a loud cheering broke out and, as Garnet was raised to her feet by the willing hand of the halberdier, the men clapped and called to each other in their enthusiasm. But Garnet was indifferent to it all. She stood quite still now, trying to regain her breath.

She stared unseeingly across at the overhanging trees at the far end of the courtyard. Let them think she was docile, a willing slave. Her owner would learn differently soon enough.

She heard a voice speaking in the foreign tongue and yet sounding familiar. Her heart began to pound and her eyes searched the sea of faces frantically. But she was foolish, suffering from the heat of the sun. She had imagined for a moment that it was Wolfe's voice, but that was impossible. He was no doubt far away, in the arms of Lucia, a traitor to all Garnet had held dear. She had long since given up any hope that Wolfe cared about her, so why should he be here, bidding for her against these rich and powerful sultans?

But he was there. He stepped out of the shadow, his face grim, his eyes silver as they met hers. He did not smile as he called another bid; he did not even acknowledge that they knew each other.

There was a pain growing within her as realization dawned. Wolfe was the man who wished to buy her for the house of ill fame. None of the sultans would find any need for such a place; they were all rich in women, wives and concubines and bondservants by the score.

In that moment, she hated him. What more could Wolfe do to her feelings of love for him?

He had won. The rest of the bidding had stopped and Wolfe went forward to Sulimary Ali and handed him a purse of gold. As Garnet watched, Wolfe took a brooch in the shape of a salamander from his pocket and, with a bow, gave that also to the sultan, who flung back his head and laughed.

The halberdier drew Garnet from the dais and took her to where Sulimary Ali sat. He leaned forward, smiling down at her.

'I have received a goodly price for you,' he said. His gaze fell upon the rich jewellery she wore. 'You may keep the baubles. My kadin gives them from her own casket,' he said grudgingly.

Wolfe was already outside the great walls, untying the reins of a stallion from the branches of an acacia tree. She stared at him with burning eyes, even as he turned to lift her into the saddle.

'And what do you want from me this time, Wolfe,' she said bitterly. 'To work for you in a whore house, is that my future? Not only did you abandon me to my own fate but then you have the arrogance to collect me like a lost parcel when I can be of use to you.'

His face was grim as he swung up behind her and slapped the animal into a gallop. Garnet was forced to lean back against him and she closed her eyes in pain.

'What happened, did Lucia grow tired of you?' she asked, her voice harsh.

'No, she did not,' he spoke for the first time and his voice was without expression. If she had not known

better, she might have thought he was hurt. He took a
deep breath, his arms tightening around her waist.

'I know you have suffered a great deal, Garnet.' He
said softly. 'But perhaps I can help you to forget all the
hardships and give you a more pleasant life.'

'Oh, yes,' she said in anger. 'By putting me in a
whore house where any man can buy my services for a
few pieces of silver. Perhaps you hope to profit on what
you paid for me at the auction, is that it?'

'Very well,' he said. 'You are determined not to
listen to what I have to say; it is obvious there is no
trust on your part. You readily believe the worst of me
without even giving me the chance to explain. There's
nothing more to be said.'

The horse was taking a downward path towards the
sea, head straining against the reins, feet slipping in
the loose soil and stones. Garnet was silent, wondering
in bewilderment how it was that Wolfe made her feel
guilty when it was he who had callously sent her
ashore at Tangiers, leaving her to fend for herself,
without a penny piece to call her own.

She saw spread out before her the glittering azure
ocean and a small sense of happiness invaded the
gloom inside her. At least he had come for her. He
must have encountered considerable difficulties in trying to find where she had been taken. But the question
was, what did he intend doing with her now?

She glanced up at his set face from beneath her
lashes. A wave of love swept over her, she wanted to
hold his face between her hands, to kiss away his frown
and see his eyes light up with happiness. She almost

made a move to touch him but he was swinging the horse towards the bay, his eyes narrowed as he looked out to sea, apparently searching for something.

On the horizon was a sailing ship, masts unfurled as though she was ready to go out with the tide. Wolfe took a mirror from his pocket and flashed a signal seawards. A pinpoint of light answered him and he sank down on a rock, his head bent, his arms resting on his knees.

Garnet stared at him. He looked tired and she wanted to put her arms around him and hold him close, tell him she loved him whatever he'd done.

'What about the story you told Sulimary Ali?' She forced herself to speak, though her heart was beating rapidly and she was afraid he would not answer her.

'About the house of ill fame?' He smiled grimly. 'It was the most feasible excuse I could think of for buying you. Your sultan would not understand that I was spending all my money on a woman he had owned as a bondslave.'

Garnet put her hand to her mouth. 'You don't think that he . . .' she paused, 'that I slept in his bed?'

His eyes stared at her strangely. 'I'm not blaming you,' he said.

'But Wolfe, you're wrong. I was not fat enough. I did not find favour with him. I was a novelty, nothing more. He did not even like me once he had a good look at me, that is why he sold me so quickly.'

Wolfe shrugged. 'It makes no difference now, don't worry. I am going to return you to England. I am not quite as bad as you seem to think I am.'

He rose to his feet as a small boat bumped against the sand. The sailor waved to them and Wolfe gestured to Garnet.

'Go along, get into the boat, I shall only be a minute.' She watched him take the reins of the horse and walk across the beach. She ached to run to him, to tell him that she forgave him everything if only he would love her. But she turned and, wrapping her cloak around her, climbed into the rowing boat opposite the cheerful sailor.

'Good day to you, Mistress Surbiton.' The man's voice was warm and with a soft English sound and Garnet smiled at him. She was still watching Wolfe as he handed over the reins of the horse to a man in loose robes who stood at the edge of the bay.

'Fine man your husband, mistress,' the sailor continued. 'I'm Jack Willis, first mate, and I came for you myself because I'm that proud to know you.'

Garnet looked at him in surprise and he laughed.

'Oh, we've all heard how Mr. Surbiton paid one of the Spanish officers to take you to friends of yours, a Mr. Summers, wasn't it? Just out beyond Tangiers there. And we all felt for your husband when he half killed the man because he took the money and just abandoned you to that scoundel Maynard.'

Garnet was suddenly warm. She felt the rich colour rise to her cheeks, she could not believe she was hearing him correctly.

'Wolfe paid the officer to take me back to Jonathon Summers' home?' she asked incredulously. She sank back in her seat, staring unseeingly at the clear sparkling sea. How she had misjudged Wolfe! No wonder he was bitterly angry with her.

'I hope Mr. Surbiton won't be too long giving that horse back to its owner,' Jack Willis said anxiously. 'We shall be setting sail within the hour, for England.'

Wolfe was running across the sand, his hair lifting in the breeze, his long legs covering the distance quickly and easily. In a few minutes, he was at the edge of the water, pushing the boat out to sea and leaping in beside Garnet.

She wanted to say so much to him, but the words stuck in her throat. He was stern, unapproachable, as he stared toward the ship that was nearer at every stroke of the oar. He was her husband and yet he seemed a stranger.

Once on board the *Devon Sands*, Wolfe directed Garnet to her cabin. Set out on the bunk was a pale cream gown of soft silk with short puffed sleeves and a satin bow to tie beneath her breasts. She quickly cast off her pantaloons and the smock and waistcoat, the last reminder of her weeks in the seraglio, and drew on the gown that was all the more precious because she knew that Wolfe had bought it for her.

She combed the tangles from her hair and then stood, undecided, staring out of the window, seeing, perhaps for the last time, the long stretch of African coast, shimmering under the sun.

The sails cracked and, as the timbers creaked, Garnet knew the journey home had begun. She started nervously as the door opened and Wolfe entered the cabin, his eyes running over her as she stood before him in the simple gown, her hair hanging over her shoulders.

She wanted to say she loved him but her courage failed her. She looked into his grey eyes and slowly held out her hand to him.

It seemed an eternity later when his fingers, strong and bronzed, curled warmly around hers. Garnet did not know who was the first to move, but then she was held against him and his heart was beating as swiftly as was her own.

She reached up her hands and touched his face, unable to believe that all this was real. His mouth came down slowly, possessing her lips, and there was no need for words. They clung together, holding each other tightly, as the *Devon Sands* cut a path through the sun-splashed water, taking them home.